The
Rebel's Return

Susan Correll Foy

Cover by Mary C. Findley

Cover photo of model Gretchen Lort courtesy of Nick Fisher

Books by Susan Correll Foy:

Finding Father
Kerry's Calling
The Rebel's Return

ℬ Chapter One ℭ

It *truly wasn't a lie*, Phoebe told herself for the fifth time as she scurried along the cobbled streets of the city. The smoldering July sun beat through the blanket of clouds that attempted to suffocate it and radiated back up from the pavement in waves; the air lay heavy and breezeless. It truly wasn't a lie, for she had just delivered the little vial of medicine to Mrs. Audley, just as she had told Martha she intended to do before leaving home. And if she returned home by way of the State House, and happened to meet her friend Rhoda on the way, and then lingered just for a moment to see what was happening there, was that truly so dreadful? Not the whole truth, perhaps, but not a lie, and she would certainly confess exactly where she had been when she returned home, whatever the consequences.

The rationalization soothed, but did not entirely silence, the little niggling of her conscience. She knew why she had told the servant about her intended errand instead of asking her mother's permission; she knew full well what her mother's response would have been. Old Mrs. Audley wasn't about to die, Sarah Fuller would have said. The poor woman had been suffering from the gout for years, as everyone knew, but she wasn't dying, and she could manage to wait one more day for her medicine. No hurry in that. Today was washday, and they needed all available hands, and once the wash was laid out to dry there were those strawberries that needed to be made into preserves before they spoiled. Not a day to be running off with Rhoda Kirby, meddling in nonsense that Phoebe had no business worrying her head over. A woman's place was in the home, after all, and speeches, war, and politics were men's concerns.

Phoebe rounded the corner of Chestnut Street and slowed her frantic trot to a walk. Several blocks ahead she could see a crowd beginning to gather in front of the State House, a milling, swaying mass of movement and color. A gentleman in a curled wig and knee breeches cantered past Phoebe, his horse kicking up a cloud of dust that made her pause, cough, and rub her eyes. The door of a shop ahead of her flew open and a trio of boys ran out, apprentices by the appearance of them, she guessed. She wondered if she would be the only woman in the crowd. Nay, at least Rhoda would be there.

Suddenly aware of her dusty, sweaty hands and face, she paused and groped in her pocket for her handkerchief. No handkerchief. How could she have forgotten? And she was still wearing the faded, patched linsey-woolsey petticoat she always wore on washday, and the waistcoat with the hole in one elbow and the grease spot on the bodice. Well, perhaps she would not see anyone she knew, or anyone besides Rhoda. But her mother was sure to notice and comment on her bedraggled, unladylike appearance.

Another sin for my Naughty Book, she reflected with a wry grimace. When Phoebe was a little girl, her mother had made her keep a record of her daily faults in a book, and ask forgiveness for them all each evening before bed. The same offenses appeared each day with monotonous, discouraging regularity. Daydreaming. Forgetting her chores. Playing when she should have been working. Reading frivolous books instead of instructional ones. Giggling during solemn moments, like in church or when being introduced to important people. Her older sister Alice also had a Naughty Book, but somehow its pages were always wonderfully white and clean. And even though ten years had passed and the two sisters were now grown, that aspect of their natures had not changed at all.

Just yesterday she had been engrossed in Samuel Richardson's novel *Pamela, or Virtue Rewarded,* the story of a brave young servant girl resisting the wicked advances of her handsome young master. Phoebe had reached the most suspenseful moment of the book, when Mr. B carries Pamela off to his country estate where she is secluded from the world, and even her shoes are stolen by the nasty housekeeper to prevent her from running away. Would Pamela finally succumb to Mr. B's seduction, or would she perhaps be rescued by the local clergyman who finds her charming? Phoebe had to find out, she simply couldn't put the book down, and she was lost to the world when her mother came upon her in the storage room.

"Are you reading that foolish book again, Phoebe?" Sarah had exclaimed, while Phoebe hastily hid the volume in her pocket under her petticoat. "Gracious, if you must waste time reading, at least choose something useful and instructional, like Alice does. Alice, dear, where is that book you were reading last week, about Elizabeth in her holy retirement?"

"I read that already," Phoebe said. *And it was gloomy*, she added silently, so her mother would not hear her. Elizabeth, preparing for the birth of her baby and meditating upon the likelihood of her own demise, was enough to frighten any young woman out of matrimony, unlike the amorous, seductive Mr. B.

"Did you indeed? Well, we're too busy today to waste time with books anyway. The garden needs weeding, and then you can cut out some new shirts for Jonathan. Your brothers grow so quickly I can't keep clothes on them."

Phoebe meekly retreated and headed for the garden to weed, but as soon as she was positioned on the ground, with her back to the house, she retrieved the book from her pocket and propped it open with her knee, so that she could read and weed at the same time. Of course the task took much longer that way, and her mother finally called out to scold her impatiently.

You know I don't mean to be wicked, Lord, she prayed silently. *You know I want to do right, but all my inclinations seem to lie in the opposite direction.*

Her reflections on her past sins were swallowed up in anticipation and excitement as she approached the swelling crowd in front of the State House. The bells of the city were ringing, calling the population to assemble, and the bell over the State House clanged ever louder as Phoebe drew near. The most important building in Philadelphia, and therefore in the whole thirteen colonies, for Philadelphia was the biggest and most important city in America. The building where the

Congress had been meeting for weeks now, all the great men of the colonies: John Adams, Thomas Jefferson, John Hancock, and of course their own Benjamin Franklin. Phoebe had occasionally lingered outside on the street when she happened to pass by, watching as these leading citizens emerged from their solemn assembly, wondering what it would be like to be so splendid and important, changing history with her own hands. She sometimes liked to imagine that she was the wife or daughter of such a man, hearing in intimate detail all the debate and contention that occurred within. But when she had confided this daydream to her sister, Alice responded with a wrinkle of her pretty nose, "How tedious! And I don't doubt those men's wives think so, too."

Now she paused on the edge of the milling crowd, searching left and right for Rhoda or someone in the Kirby family. She saw working men in checked shirts and woolen caps and aprons, kerchiefs round their necks, apprentices with laughing servant girls hanging on their arms, occasionally a young man in soldier's uniform, although most of those were far away, in New York with the army. A holiday spirit pervaded the crowd, with a sense of anticipation and expectancy. Then she heard Rhoda's voice behind her, calling her name, and she turned.

"I feared you would miss everything!" Rhoda seized her arm and drew her away from the press of bodies. "I heard Mr. Jones tell my father that John Nixon, the commander of the Philadelphia city guard, will be coming out in just a few moments to speak to everyone. And I couldn't find you anywhere."

"I had difficulty getting away," Phoebe explained. "I nearly didn't come at all."

"Did no one in your family come with you?" Rhoda glanced around behind them. She was a pretty sort of girl, almost as short as Phoebe but plumper, with glossy dark hair, bright eyes, and pink cheeks.

"They didn't know where I was going, and I'm sure they would have been too busy to come if I'd told them. Today is washday, you see."

"They don't realize how important this is," Rhoda declared, and Phoebe, torn between loyalty to her family and agreement with her friend, was once again struck by the difference between her family and Rhoda's. Rhoda's father was a member of the Associators, marching companies composed of Philadelphia merchants, clerks, printers, and other city folk. Rhoda's two older brothers were with the army in New York, and even her two younger ones, eleven and thirteen years old, drilled as drummer boys with the Associators. Phoebe's family in contrast cared little for politics. Her quiet, withdrawn father, after a bad bout with pneumonia several years before, now devoted himself only to his apothecary shop and his Bible reading, even maintaining few social contacts among his former acquaintances. Her mother was the one who really ran the family, and her concerns were physical ones, food and drink, health and cleanliness, running the family business, and finding husbands for her two marriageable daughters. Or they were moral concerns, honesty and virtue and hard work. The political issues of the day interested her not at all, except peripherally, as they affected her own family. And Alice, as diligent as her mother and as devout as her father, found nothing so tiresome as politics.

"If George were at home, he would have come with me," Phoebe said. But George was also far away with Washington's army in New York. Just over six months ago he had come home and announced his intention to turn soldier, much to the distress of his mother. Why should he waste his time and risk his life for some silly cause that was lost before it was even fought, when his father needed him in the apothecary shop? Surely he knew his family was depending on him. But uncharacteristically George's father had intervened.

"Let him go, Sarah," he'd said quietly. "'Tis where his heart is. You can't keep him tied to you forever." So George had marched off to join the army in New York, although his mother remained convinced he would be blown to bits by the next cannon ball.

"I thought surely Alice would come, when I saw Edmund Ingram here," Rhoda said.

"Edmund is here?" Phoebe exclaimed, glancing around the crowded yard. "I'm sure Alice didn't know he was coming; at least, she didn't mention it. Where is he?"

Rhoda shrugged. "I don't know; perhaps he has left by now."

Phoebe did not reply, but twisted left and right, scanning the crowd for Edmund, her sister's beau. They had been courting for several months now, and in Phoebe's opinion Edmund embodied all the qualities of an ideal young man, a view largely shared by the rest of her family. Tall and slender, graceful of movement and erect of carriage, with dark hair, fine eyes, and good teeth. Rather quiet and reserved, but intelligent. His family, although not wealthy, had scraped together enough to send him to the College of New Jersey so he could become a lawyer—a comfortable step up the social ladder. He would be a good catch for Alice, and Alice was nearly perfect enough to deserve him. But Phoebe was surprised to hear that Rhoda had seen him in the crowd, for he had never displayed interest in politics or in the current rebellion.

She was distracted from her search by a movement near the door of the State House. She tried to peer over the heads of the men in front of her to see what was happening, but she was too short. Rhoda nudged her. "John Nixon," she whispered.

A hush spread over the crowd, beginning at the front and spreading backwards like the ripples of a stone in a pond. Phoebe, still standing on tiptoe, missed his first remarks, but then the silence deepened, and the words rang out over the people like the solemn sounding of a bell. He was reading from the text in his hand.

"When in the Course of human events, it becomes necessary for one people to dissolve the political bands which have connected them with another, and to assume among the powers of the earth, the separate and equal station to which the Laws of Nature and of Nature's God entitle them, a decent respect to the opinions of mankind requires that they should declare the causes which impel them to the separation.—We hold these truths to be self-evident, that all men are created equal, that they are endowed by their Creator with certain unalienable Rights, that among these are Life, Liberty and the pursuit of Happiness."

Phoebe felt a chill go through her at the words. She suddenly squeezed Rhoda's arm, and her friend flashed her a smile.

"—That whenever any Form of Government becomes destructive to these ends, it is the Right of the People to alter or to abolish it, and to institute new Government, laying its foundation on such principles and organizing its powers in such form, as to them shall seem most likely to effect their Safety and Happiness. Prudence, indeed, will dictate that Governments long established should not be changed for light and transient causes..."

Throughout the course of her life, Phoebe would hear the Declaration of Independence read many times, and each time it would carry her back to this day, the hot summer haze, the still air, the smell of grime and sweat on the hushed and breathless crowd, each standing on tiptoe lest the words be swallowed up by those in front of them. She listened solemnly to the long list of the crimes of the King, and then the ringing conclusion.

"—We, THEREFORE, the Representatives of the united States of America, in General Congress, Assembled, appealing to the Supreme Judge of the world for the rectitude of our intentions, do, in the Name, and by the Authority of the good People of these Colonies, solemnly publish and declare, That these United Colonies are, and of Right ought to be FREE AND INDEPENDENT STATES;... And for the support of this Declaration, with a firm reliance on the protection of divine Providence, we mutually pledge to each other our Lives, our Fortunes, and our sacred Honor."

For a lingering instant after the reading had concluded, the silence hovered over the crowd, as if each individual expelled his long-held breath in unison. Then all at once a great cheer broke out among the throng. Men threw their caps in the air, women hugged one another, and here and there pistol shots rang out from the uniformed soldiers.

There! Phoebe thought triumphantly. *There! We made history, and I was part of it, in however small a way. But for how long? Can we really survive apart from Great Britain?* She thought of the ragtag army in New York, her own brother and Rhoda's brothers, facing the might of a world power. It was a fearful picture. And was it even right to rebel against the king? She knew what the Bible taught about obedience to the government and other authorities. Her parents had taught her well in childhood, and she had read the passages herself as an adult. When was it proper to submit, and when was rebellion the correct response to tyranny and injustice?

"Can you tarry?" Rhoda asked, raising her voice slightly to be heard over the cheering voices. "My father said Mr. Jones brought a whole keg of cider to share, and there will be games this afternoon."

Phoebe was sorely tempted, but the image of her mother's ire returned her sense of the responsibility. "I cannot." She shook her head with a sigh. "I've been gone too long already."

Rhoda frowned but did not argue. Phoebe waved farewell to her friend and began to weave her way to the entrance of the yard. She had to elbow past clusters of young men in high spirits, one of them slightly tipsy, too preoccupied to move aside for the shabbily dressed young woman. Unwilling to call attention to herself, Phoebe tried to squeeze between two noisy groups, and as she ducked under their elbows, she ran smack into an officer's uniform coming the other way.

"Excuse me, sir," Phoebe mumbled, trying to slip past him without looking up.

"Phoebe?" the male voice said. "Phoebe Fuller?"

Startled, Phoebe raised her eyes from the row of coat buttons to the man's face. She saw a young man of about twenty-five, a tanned, rather square face, wavy brown hair sun-streaked with blond, pulled back and tied at the nape with a blue ribbon. His eyes were a sparkling hazel, laughing eyes. Not tall, she judged, no more than average height or a bit less, but still a good eight inches taller than Phoebe, who was small for a woman.

"Nicholas!" She recognized him now. His family had once lived on the same street as the Fuller family, until his father accumulated enough from his trade to purchase a country estate, raising the family to the status of gentry. His sister Lavinia had been Phoebe's best friend when they were both children.

"How many years has it been?" Nicholas asked. "I remember you as a tiny girl—I barely recognized you."

"I don't know; these six years at least." Phoebe rubbed her palms against her petticoat, suddenly conscious of her grimy appearance.

She was jostled from behind, and Nicholas grasped her arm and pulled her aside to a quieter corner of the yard.

"This is a rather rough crowd for you, Phoebe. Did your family let you come alone? "

"Nay, I—I sneaked out."

She regretted the words as soon as they were out of her mouth, but he laughed heartily, his eyes narrowing and crinkling at the corners.

"So how old are you now? Fifteen?"

Phoebe swallowed hard and looked away. She knew, of course, that she was barely the same height as her ten-year-old brother Kit, with a figure only slightly more developed. She knew that her movements were quick as a bird's, not graceful as a young lady's should be, that her voice was often too high-pitched, and that her countenance displayed her every emotion like the changes of a kaleidoscope. She knew all these undignified facts about herself, yet she was still mortified every time a stranger thought her much younger than she actually was.

She said in a voice that she hoped sounded normal, "I'm eighteen."

"Indeed!" His face reddened just for a moment with chagrin before he recovered. "Aye, indeed you are, I should have remembered. You were friends with Lavinia, and she will be eighteen in November."

Phoebe smiled up at him, hoping to dispel his embarrassment. "Everyone thinks I am younger than I am."

"You will be pleased by that someday," he assured her with a grin. "Do you still hear from Lavinia?"

She shook her head with an expression of regret. "Not these two or three years. We used to write, even to visit, then we lost touch. Are your family all well?"

He shrugged slightly. "They were well the last time I saw them. And yours? I believe I saw George once with the army in New York."

She smiled with pride. "Aye, he is with Washington's army. As you are as well, I see. Are you an officer?"

"I am a lieutenant under Lord Stirling, but I ride courier for whoever needs me. Which is why I find myself in Philadelphia now, actually. How lucky, to be here today of all days! Although I'm sure the Declaration will be read to the army as well."

"Aye, it is so exciting," Phoebe agreed with a glowing countenance, but as she glanced over her companion's shoulder she was suddenly distracted by a familiar figure on the edge of the crowd. "Why, there's Edmund, after all!"

"Who?" Nicholas twisted around to follow the direction of her gaze. "You know him?"

"Aye, Edmund Ingram, Alice's beau. They have been keeping company several months now."

"I see." Nicholas studied the figure thoughtfully and then turned back to Phoebe. "Would I be imposing if I escorted you home? I should like to renew my acquaintance with your family."

Phoebe forgot to conceal her eagerness. "I'm sure they would all be very happy to see you again, sir."

He grinned at that, then took her arm in a commanding way and led her out of the State House yard and into the street toward her home. As they walked she told him about her ploy to escape the house that day, and her fear of her mother's reproach.

"Perhaps with a guest present she won't scold you so much," he suggested.

Phoebe sighed. "Aye, I hope not."

A carriage dashed by, and as it passed drove through a mud puddle, splattering them both with mud. Phoebe exclaimed in disgust and jumped backwards.

"How rude," Nicholas frowned. He turned and, following the carriage a few steps, suddenly pulled his pistol from his pocket and fired it into the air. The carriage horses began to neigh and rear, and as heads turned on the street Nicholas calmly replaced his pistol and strolled back to join Phoebe.

"Nicholas!" Phoebe exclaimed, torn between laughter and horror. "Why did you do that?"

"Next time he'll watch his manners," Nicholas grinned, and in spite of herself she had to laugh.

They reached the Fuller house after a fifteen minute walk. Phoebe paused with her hand on the latch, wondering if she could sneak back to her chores without her mother noticing. But with Nicholas that would be impossible. She took a breath and lifted the latch.

The cloying smell of strawberries and sugar met her nose as she and Nicholas stepped into the parlor, dark to Phoebe's eyes after the bright afternoon sun. Her father's desk stood against one wall with the finer chairs that the family owned, and Alice's harpsichord held the place of honor on the other side. The kitchen door opened and her mother's head appeared in the doorway.

"Phoebe! So you're finally back! Whatever possessed you to deliver that medicine today when you know we have all these strawberries—" She broke off as her gaze fell on Nicholas, and recognition dawned. She opened the door wider and stepped into the parlor. "My goodness! Is that Nicholas Teasdale? What a surprise!"

Nicholas removed his cap and bowed. "I met your daughter on her errand in town and she was kind enough to invite me to call on the family."

"How lovely! It is so good to see you again. It has been so long since I've heard from your good mother! How is your family? I hope you left them in good health?"

"I believe so. It has been awhile since I have heard from them myself. I am with the army in New York, at the disposal of my superiors. I haven't been home since last summer."

"Of course. What a fine uniform you have. I'm sure George is not wearing anything half so grand. Alice," she turned back to call through the kitchen door, "we have a guest. You'll never imagine. Come and see if you recognize him."

Alice appeared in the parlor, missing the large apron she wore on workdays, her petticoat fresh and clean. Phoebe knew she had discarded the apron quickly at the voice of a guest in the parlor. She wished she could run upstairs and change her own clothes, but it was too late for that.

She glanced swiftly up at Nicholas and saw his eyes light up at the sight of her pretty sister.

"Of course I remember," Alice greeted him with a laugh. "All the mischief you made as a little boy! How could I forget the time you stole the gingerbread I had baked for company and ate it all? I found the empty pan full of crumbs in the kitchen window."

Nicholas bowed again. "I hope you have forgiven me for that. I would be grieved to think that my childhood sins are making me unwelcome today. As I recall, it was very good gingerbread." His tone was serious, but, stealing a glance at him, Phoebe saw that his eyes were dancing.

They all laughed. Sarah Fuller asked, "How long can you stay? If you could join us for supper, my husband would have a chance to visit with you too. I know he would enjoy that."

"I fear I can't tarry today. My duties call me elsewhere. But please give your husband my greetings. Perhaps I will see him another time."

"You must be sure to call on us whenever you are in Philadelphia."

"Indeed, I would be very pleased to," he assured her. "I have to pass through Philadelphia often in my duties, and it would be pleasant to have friends to visit."

"I hope you will consider our house your second home," Sarah said. And Phoebe found herself unaccountably happy at the thought of Nicholas frequently dropping by.

80 CB

That night the events of the day were still replaying in Phoebe's mind even after she had undressed down to her shift and snuggled under the sheet of the bed she shared with Alice. Two adventures in one day! Hearing independence declared, and then meeting Nicholas! She did not often enjoy so much excitement at once.

She watched now as Alice unhooked her petticoats and slipped out of them, then unpinned her hair and began to brush it out. Alice had a perfect figure, neither tall nor short, straight and graceful. She wore her corsets to bed, while Phoebe often tried to escape without hers even in the daytime. Alice's hair, unpinned, fell to her waist, and shone in the candlelight, pure gold. Phoebe's own hair was almost brown, with streaks of silver-gold that showed up only in the sunlight.

She rolled onto her back, staring up at the rafters moodily. Nicholas had seemed quite struck by Alice's beauty that afternoon. Could it be that he planned to visit the family to see more of her?

Aloud, she said, "I wonder if Nicholas will return soon."

"I don't know," Alice replied, not looking around. "He said he planned to."

"He's very good-looking, don't you think?" Phoebe asked wistfully.

"Not exactly." Alice began to rapidly pin up her hair. "He's too short. His brother Philip was the handsome one, if I remember rightly."

Phoebe turned to stare at her. "He's not short! He's taller than you are."

Alice shrugged. "To my mind a man is not really tall if I can look him in the eye."

Phoebe digested this in silence. To be sure, Nicholas was not as tall as Edmund, and his features were not so perfect and regular. But he was still attractive. Alice was so beautiful that she could afford to be very choosy. And yet, even as she spurned them, the men kept pursuing her. What would it be like to be Alice, to never anger her mother, to never neglect her duties, to attract men without even trying? Phoebe sighed. She would never know, for she would surely never be Alice.

❧ *Chapter Two* ❧

Nicholas returned the next day at tea-time, and two days later in the evening. He would be in Philadelphia for a few weeks on a particular errand, he said, and he hoped they would not tire of his presence before he needed to rejoin the army in New York. He addressed these remarks in particular to Alice, and she assured him he would always be welcome in the Fuller household. Indeed, as the week passed and his visits continued, he gave more and more of his attention to Alice, and in spite of her earlier comments to Phoebe, Alice did not appear to find his company irksome. Of course, Alice was always a perfect lady; she would never wear her heart on her sleeve as Phoebe often did, and she would never lower herself to flirt, or anything so vulgar. Still, watching the two of them together, Phoebe had to conclude that Nicholas would not be completely unreasonable if he decided that his attentions to Alice were welcome.

Edmund Ingram also continued to call on Alice, but fortunately for both men and especially for Alice, they had never yet chosen the same evening to come courting. Phoebe knew Nicholas was aware of Edmund's existence, for she had told him herself, and wondered when Edmund would discover that he had a rival.

Toward the end of July Nicholas came for supper and as he visited with the family, he told them that he would be leaving the next day for New York. Phoebe felt her heart drop in her chest and hoped her feelings were not displayed on her face. She glanced at Alice, but her sister was polite and smiling as always.

"We're sorry you have to leave," she said, "especially with a war going on. That must be frightening."

"When is the war going to start?" demanded Jonathan, a tall husky boy of twelve. "I wish I could go off and fight."

Sarah threw an alarmed glance over her shoulder as she rose to refill the pitcher in her hands. "Nonsense! You're much too young! It's bad enough that your brother wanted to turn soldier."

Nicholas smiled at the boy. "He's no smaller than some of the drummer boys with the army now. But no, Jonathan," seeing Sarah's expression, "you'd better stay at home till you're a little older. Your mother would worry. Unfortunately, the war won't likely be over before you have your chance."

"He's big for his age," Sarah returned, "but he's too young. I don't want him to get any ideas."

She began to clear the table, stacking pewter plates with little bangs and thumps, and Phoebe rose to join her. The males of the family filed out of the kitchen.

"I need to take leave of you now, Mrs. Fuller," Nicholas said. "Thank you for your hospitality these last few weeks, and for this fine supper."

He smiled at Sarah and then at Phoebe, a quick, engaging, mischievous smile with those little crinkles around his eyes. Phoebe smiled in return. She saw him speak softly to Alice, and the two of them disappeared through the door together. Phoebe bit her lip, swallowed hard, and began to fill the basin with hot water from the fire.

She couldn't blame Nicholas for choosing Alice as the object of his interest. It was surely the most natural thing in the world, and although she could not observe the developing relationship without a few pangs, they were pangs of sadness rather than resentment.

I suppose Nicholas is not for me, Lord, she prayed silently as she began scrubbing the plates and cups. In these last few weeks, he had never once distinguished her by any particular attention. *Lord, I suppose this means there is another man for me somewhere—if I ever do marry, that is—and after all, I don't know Nicholas very well. He is attractive and charming, but that doesn't mean he is the sort of godly husband that I would want.*

She resolved to put Nicholas out of her mind—at least while he was out of town—and was assisted in this worthy resolution at the end of July by another unexpected arrival. The family was gathered around the supper table one evening when they heard the front door open without a knock, then heavy footsteps in the hall. Sarah called sharply, "Who is that?" and Phoebe exclaimed, "George is home!" just as her brother burst through the kitchen door.

There were cries and embraces all around, beginning with her mother, followed by Phoebe and her little sister Sally. Alice rose to offer her brother a light kiss, and her father gave him a quiet smile and patted his back as he joined the family around the table.

"Here, fill your plate, you must be hungry after your trip," Sarah told him, bustling to bring the platter of turnips and the pot of lentil soup. "Sally, run and fetch your brother a cup of buttermilk; he's thirsty. Surely you didn't walk all the way from New York?"

"Nay, and I'm thankful, for that would have used up my whole leave, and I'd need to turn right around as soon as I got here." George laughed as he broke off a hunk of bread and lathered it with thick yellow butter. "I was fortunate enough to meet up with a trader a few miles outside of New York, who offered me a ride in his wagon for a few shillings. But now I'm completely penniless, and half-starved to boot. I can't remember when I've tasted anything so good," he added, gulping down the soup with relish.

"You look thinner," his mother frowned with a crease between her eyes. "We'll need to fatten you up while you're home, and send you back with something to keep your soul in your body, if such a thing is possible."

Phoebe thought her brother looked thinner too, and altered in a way that had little to do with nourishment. He seemed leaner, tougher, harder. Perhaps a soldier's life changed a man that way.

"Tell us about the war, George," piped up Jonathan, and Kit added, "Did you shoot any redcoats?"

"Not yet." His brother gulped his mouthful of soup. "But I'll likely have an opportunity soon enough. We've been digging fortifications all over Manhattan and on Brooklyn Heights, and Admiral Howe arrived with his fleet just this month. They want to blast us out of New York, and it will come to fighting within weeks, I reckon."

Phoebe saw a sudden look of fear cross her mother's face.

"Especially now that the Congress has signed that foolish Declaration of Independence. Gracious, what were they thinking of? The King will never forgive us for that."

"We had to do it, Mother. There's no reconciling with England now; things have gone too far. But New York is so full of Tories, the British will no doubt feel right at home there, if they ever get in, that is."

Phoebe leaned toward her brother, her eyes alight. "You'll shoot them down the same way they did at Bunker Hill."

"Aye, I hope so. That was a great battle to hear everyone tell about it. I wish I had been there. But I'll surely have my own chance soon enough."

Alice shivered as she patted her mouth with her napkin. "I don't understand how anyone can be excited about fighting in a war. It sounds dreadful to me."

George grinned at her. "That's why women don't go to war. You have your own battles at home. But tell me what is happening here. Is that Ingram fellow still coming around, paying court to Alice?"

"Alice has two beaus now," Jonathan boasted. "Nicholas Teasdale has been tarrying with her as well."

"He's not my beau," Alice returned with dignity.

"He's Phoebe's beau," Kit said, and Phoebe started.

"He's no one's beau," their mother scolded, "just an old friend of the family. You remember the Teasdales, George; they used to live three houses down until they moved to the countryside. His mother was a friend of mine."

"Aye, I remember them. I've seen Nicholas in New York on a few occasions as well. He's an officer, so we aren't of the same rank, and he has a different set of friends. I believe he is connected to Lord Stirling."

The next several days were almost like a holiday, for Sarah Fuller found so much pleasure in her son's company that she abandoned all work but the most necessary chores to keep her family clothed and fed. Friends and relatives dropped by to see George, and the adults in the family went visiting more than they normally did. One day Phoebe's aunt, uncle, and cousins came for dinner and lingered for the rest of the afternoon, reminiscing over old times, playing dominoes and cribbage.

The next evening George accompanied Alice and Phoebe to a party at the home of friends, where they spent the evening singing and dancing, and returned home after midnight.

The next day George expressed an interest in visiting the Kirby family before he returned to the army, and Phoebe offered to accompany him. As they entered the Kirby house George joined the men of the family in the parlor and Rhoda's mother told Phoebe that Rhoda was upstairs in the girls' bedchamber. She climbed the steep narrow stairs to the familiar room and through the open door heard voices deep in conversation.

"I couldn't do it, Rhoda. I just couldn't marry someone my parents disapproved of. What do you think? What would you do in my situation?"

Phoebe stepped through the door of the cluttered bedroom with the two beds and the profusion of boxes and chests littering the floor. Her friend was curled up on the bed next to Tom Kirby's sweetheart, Betsy Snow. Betsy wore a troubled expression that didn't completely disappear as the two girls looked up and saw Phoebe.

"I suppose it is different for me, because my parents aren't as religious as yours," Rhoda said, speaking as freely in front of Phoebe as she normally did. "We go to church most Sundays, but my parents wouldn't care much which church I belong to. They wouldn't be bothered if I married someone from a different church." She patted the red and blue nine-patch quilt beside her in a gesture of invitation to Phoebe. "What about you, Phoebe? Would your mother object if you didn't marry someone from the Methodist society?"

Phoebe perched on the edge of the bed with the two friends, pondering the question. "I've never actually asked her. And I've never had anyone want to court me yet. Of course, my mother didn't object when Tom wanted to court Alice—" She broke off with a glance at Betsy, but Tom Kirby's new love interest seemed engrossed by her own distress and ignored the reference to Alice.

"Your parents don't care so much about religion, but they do care about politics," Betsy pointed out to Rhoda. "Just imagine if you wanted to marry a Loyalist. Wouldn't your father object to that? I'm sure he would."

"*I* would object to marrying a Tory myself," Rhoda laughed. "My father wouldn't need to say anything against it. But if I met someone I really cared for, and my parents objected to him, I'd find a way somehow, you can be sure of that. I wouldn't take no for an answer. And I really believe, if I were sure of my own mind and my parents saw that I knew what I wanted, they would agree in the end."

Betsy stretched out full length on the bed and rested her pale, pretty face in her hands. "I've always believed I should obey my parents in everything that isn't directly a matter of conscience. That's what I've always been taught. You don't agree with that?"

Rhoda leaned on her elbow, pulling her yellow petticoat down to cover her ankles. "Couldn't you say that marrying Tom is a matter of conscience?"

Betsy still frowned in spite of her friend's attempt at humor. "I don't see it that way. There's nothing in the Bible that says what person I should marry. So if my parents tell me not to marry him, shouldn't I take that as an answer from God? That my first duty is to obey my parents?" She glanced up at Phoebe as if searching for agreement. "Don't you think so, Phoebe?"

Phoebe opened her mouth to speak. It was a question she had wrestled with as well, although she had never yet needed to make such a choice.

"Don't ask Phoebe's opinion." Rhoda bounced on the straw mattress, tossing her head impatiently. "She would never do anything to upset her mother. Even if it were a matter of conscience, as you say."

Phoebe turned to her friend with an expression of surprise, bordering on indignation. "Why should you say something like that?"

Rhoda shrugged. "Don't be angry, but 'tis the truth. You're so worried about displeasing her. I can't imagine you defying her in anything."

"I think Phoebe is like me," Betsy said. "We aren't rebellious at heart. We both want to please our parents. You, Rhoda, you are much more independent."

"Nay." Rhoda shook her head. "Phoebe is different from you, Betsy. You obey your parents because you believe it is the right thing to do, because you believe God has told you to. Phoebe obeys her parents because their approval is important to her and she is afraid to lose it."

Phoebe turned to stare at Rhoda in surprise. She had never heard

Rhoda express this opinion so plainly before, although perhaps she should have guessed. She knew her friend did not mean to be critical of her, but she also knew the remark was not a compliment. Dejected, she traced the line of quilting on the bed cover with her finger.

"I think I displease my mother a lot," she frowned, "usually without trying to."

Rhoda laughed again. "That's the truth. You displease her in little things, without trying. But you would never disobey her in something really important. Like choosing a husband, for instance."

Phoebe turned to study Betsy's troubled expression with sympathy. "Your parents don't want you to marry Tom, and Rhoda thinks you should anyway."

Betsy sighed. "They like Tom. But he's a soldier and we're Quakers. I don't know what to do."

Phoebe nodded. "And I don't know what I'd do either. In your case, Betsy, maybe you need to decide whether you really agree with the Quakers in their attitude about war. Are all wars really wrong? I don't believe they are—I think there are parts of the Bible that support war. But if you believe they are, maybe you shouldn't marry Tom—if you disagree with him about something so important."

Betsy managed a weak laugh. "And that's part of my problem. When I hear my parents and the others at the Quaker Meeting talk about war, what they say makes a lot of sense. But when I talk to Tom about it, he makes sense too. How is someone like me supposed to know, when so many good and intelligent people disagree?"

The conversation moved on to the dance they had all attended the night before, and an hour later George called to Phoebe that they needed to hurry home for supper. She bade good-bye to her two friends and skipped down the stairs, her mind still full of the conversation. What was the right thing to do in Betsy's situation? And Rhoda's reflection on her character nagged at her. Of course she wanted to make her parents happy, especially her mother, who was sometimes difficult to please. Was that wrong? Would it be better to be like Rhoda, and not worry so much about it? Or to be like Alice, and please without trying?

And then there was the bigger question about war in general and this war in particular. As Betsy had said, how could Phoebe know who was correct when so many good and intelligent people disagreed? When the current rebellion was discussed in her home, her mother often reminded her that no government was perfect and they were all lucky to be English men and women. As subjects of the British crown, they were far better off than subjects of almost any other ruler, and it was their God-given duty to obey and submit instead of stirring up trouble. But then she would visit the Kirbys and listen to them talk about the rebellion with their friends. Then she would hear their indignation at the King of England, his tyrannical treatment of the citizens of Boston, his unjust taxes. It was the duty of free men to resist such treatment and to throw off the chains of tyranny, and those who refused were cowards and milksops. As for their British freedoms, they were simply demanding the rights that all free Englishmen had claimed since the Magna Carta. Listening to them, inspired by their passion, Phoebe felt sure they were right, just as her mother also seemed to make sense in her turn.

She had almost forgotten George until he spoke and interrupted her musings. As they strolled along the cobbled streets side by side, he began with a note of hesitation in his voice, "There's something I wanted to mention to you, Phoebe, if you don't mind."

"Of course not." Phoebe glanced into his face, surprised by his serious tone.

"I know Nicholas Teasdale has been calling on you when he's in town," George said. "I don't know him well, you understand, I only know him by reputation."

Phoebe felt her heart skip a beat and hoped she wasn't blushing. George knew her too well. "He doesn't have a good reputation? He's a perfect gentleman whenever he visits us."

"I certainly *hope* he acts like a gentleman in our home." George kicked a loose stone out of his way. "In an army camp, men behave differently. Not that Nicholas is the worst, compared to some of them, but...I just want you to be careful, to be wary."

"What have you heard?"

"He runs with a bit of a wild crowd. He likes to drink more than he should and— well, he socializes with women who are not exactly of the best sort."

Phoebe felt a sense of disappointment that she knew was absurd, since Nicholas was really nothing to her but a friend of the family. She digested this information in silence and finally replied, in what she hoped was an indifferent tone, "Aye, well, you needn't worry about me. He's not interested in me—he's interested in Alice."

George walked along in silence for a moment, and when Phoebe stole a glance at him, she saw him nodding to himself, as if in satisfaction. "That's well, then. Alice can take care of herself."

Phoebe shot him a hurt, reproachful look. "Alice can take care of herself—and I can't?"

"You understand what I mean, Phoebe." George laughed and rubbed his sister's shoulder affectionately. "Alice has a heart of stone. No man living could take advantage of her."

"And I'm so weak I'll fall into the arms of the first man who winks at me," Phoebe scowled.

"Not weak perhaps, but—soft, sentimental, persuadable. Someone like Nicholas could probably charm you into some indiscretion, and I want you to be careful."

"I'm not so weak as you think," Phoebe returned stiffly, and hoped she was telling the truth. It was mortifying that her brother had read her so easily, and that he had such a low opinion of her fortitude. And he knew Alice well enough to guess she would not be swept away so readily. The comparison, as usual, was humbling to her.

"He comes from a religious family," she replied after walking on for a moment in silence. "His mother was a very devout Christian, if I remember rightly, and I thought that Lavinia was too. What do they think about his behavior, if 'tis as bad as you say?"

George shrugged and sighed a bit. "They likely don't know everything that happens when he's away from home. And Nicholas isn't the first young man from a good family to go a bit wild and disappoint his parents."

"Aye, that's certain." *And all the more reason to put him from your head*, she told herself firmly. *If you want to break your heart, at least find someone worthy, someone you can look back on later in life and be proud of having loved.*

৪০ ୯୫

George returned to New York and life in the Fuller household returned to normal. One evening early in August Phoebe and Alice were sitting in the parlor sewing while their mother and Sally visited a sick member of their church and their father and the boys worked out of doors in the summer evening twilight. The windows were open to admit a faint breeze, and the silver on the cupboard reflected the fading light. Rhoda Kirby had dropped by the evening before, and Phoebe was mulling over the Kirby family dilemma as she put the finishing touches on three shirts for her brother Jonathan.

"Rhoda's brother Tom wants to marry Betsy Snow, that Quaker girl he's been courting, the next time he comes home on leave," she informed Alice. "But Betsy's parents won't consent until he joins the Quaker meeting. And he can't become a Quaker as long as he's a soldier. So he has to choose between fighting in the army and marrying Betsy. What a dilemma!"

"He doesn't have any place courting Betsy Snow in the first place." Alice bit off the thread on her needle and tied the ends.

For a moment Phoebe fell silent, taken aback. "You think it is wrong for him to marry a Quaker?"

Alice snipped off a new length of thread and held it up to the eye of the needle. "He should choose his church based on his own convictions, not on trying to please some girl's parents."

Phoebe considered for a moment. Alice was right, of course, in principle, but sometimes it was difficult to know how to put her principles into practice.

"So you think it is always wrong for people of different churches to marry?" she asked. "After all, the Quakers are Christians like we are."

"They may be Christians, but they have wrong beliefs." Her sister picked up the shirt in her lap and began to ply her needle. "Their belief in pacifism is just one example. How can Tom Kirby justify joining a church that teaches pacifism when he has served in the army for months? 'Tis nothing short of hypocrisy."

Phoebe digested this statement. Alice was completely logical and always made perfect sense, especially when she was able to discount human emotions. Perhaps it *was* hypocritical of Tom to become a Quaker if he disagreed with one of their basic tenets. Still, shouldn't there be room for a certain amount of compromise, even in matters of faith? The Fuller family was Methodist, attending the new church called St. George's, whose pulpit had recently been occupied by Francis Asbury. Phoebe liked the Methodist church, in particular the hymns, which were lively and modern, but a limited number of young men attended there. If she were to meet a man who was, for example, Presbyterian—like the Teasdale family—would it be terribly wicked of her to change churches? But she dared not voice such a heretical idea to Alice.

She shook herself to erase the thought of the Teasdales from her head. Just then she heard a knock on the door, and the footsteps of Martha, the houseservant, as she hurried to open it.

The parlor door opened and Nicholas entered.

Phoebe felt a warmth spread up and suffuse her face as Nicholas greeted the two sisters. Alice rose to welcome him and offered him a seat with perfect poise.

"What great good fortune, to find two charming young ladies home together," Nicholas exclaimed, dropping into the empty chair between them. "Not that I don't find the rest of your family charming as well, you understand."

Phoebe laughed, and then reflected silently that Nicholas might be even more pleased to find only one charming young lady. Perhaps she should leave him alone with Alice. But she was in the middle of making buttonholes on Jonathan's shirts, a tedious and painstaking business, and it would be awkward to get up and leave in the middle of her task. Not that she was eager to leave, but neither did she want to intrude her presence where she was unwelcome.

She was relieved when Nicholas struck up a conversation that included both of them, relating the latest news of the war and his own plans. He was only stopping in Philadelphia tonight in order to deliver several messages, and would return to New York the next day. As he spoke he noticed Phoebe's volume of *Pamela, or Virtue Rewarded* lying on the table, picked it up, and leafed through it idly.

He grinned at Phoebe. "I see you are an admirer of Samuel Richardson."

"How—how did you know it was mine?" she exclaimed in confusion.

"For some reason I didn't believe it was the type of book Alice would read."

Of course, he would realize that immediately. "'Tis a frivolous book, I know," she blushed, wishing she had hidden it in her room.

"I must confess, I read a bit of it myself years ago. Not the whole book. I just skipped through until I found the bawdy scenes."

Phoebe blushed deeper, but had to laugh. "Don't you think it has an exciting story?"

"In more ways than one," he agreed. "That Mr. B was quite a naughty fellow, wasn't he?"

"But he improved greatly in the end," Phoebe pointed out.

Nicholas glanced down at the volume in his hands, then shrugged and tossed it back onto the table. "The conclusion was not terribly realistic."

"You believe that virtue is never rewarded?"

"Aye, perhaps it is, more often than I might wish," he laughed. "I suppose you believe men can be changed by the love of a good woman."

"I don't know." Phoebe hesitated, on less familiar ground now. "I know God is the only one who can change people. But Pamela trusted God and did what she knew to be right, and perhaps Mr. B admired her for that."

She saw him smile at that, a bit sardonically she thought, and wondered if she had said something terribly naïve and silly. "Richardson wrote a second book that didn't end quite so romantically. Have you ever read *Clarissa*? Her lover was even wickeder than Pamela's."

"I beg you not to encourage Phoebe to read more of those books," Alice interposed. "She already neglects all her serious studies to read novels instead. Her French would be better than mine if she studied more, for she has a better memory, but she doesn't apply herself."

Nicholas turned to Alice with deference. "All of us would do well to employ our time as conscientiously as you do, Mistress Alice," he said gravely, but Phoebe thought she discerned a twitch in the corner of his mouth, and when he glanced back at Phoebe, he winked.

They were distracted from their conversation by another knock at the door, and a moment later Edmund Ingram entered the parlor.

Phoebe glanced swiftly at Alice. She perceived that her sister blushed very slightly and seemed just momentarily disconcerted, but she recovered her composure in an instant and introduced the two men, who bowed very politely to each other.

It was now absolutely necessary for Phoebe to remain, for leaving Alice alone with two men would be awkward beyond belief. Edmund took a seat on the far side of Alice and instantly commanded her attention, and to Phoebe's joy Nicholas turned and devoted his attention to her. He began to speak again about the army, describing in detail the fortifications and the numbers of regiments, the locations of each and the plans for battle with the British. Phoebe was a bit surprised by his choice of a topic. Most men would not consider a young woman to be fascinated by military strategy and wondered why he believed she would be. Perhaps he couldn't think of anything more interesting to discuss. At any rate, she was too pleased by his notice to feel terribly critical, and found his description of Fort Washington nearly as interesting as he seemed to consider it.

Finally, after chatting on in this manner for about twenty minutes, Nicholas said he needed to leave, rose, and bade farewell to the three of them. Phoebe finished the buttonhole she was working on, and, deciding that chaperoning Alice and Edmund was more tedium than she cared to submit herself to, rose to go to the kitchen where she heard her mother clattering around. But as she started toward the door she noticed a paper lying by the parlor door and picked it up.

It was a letter, addressed to Robert Morris of the Secret Committee of Congress in Philadelphia.

"I think Nicholas must have dropped this," she said to the other two, frowning. "He likely intended to deliver it tonight. What should we do?"

Edmund broke off in the middle of his sentence and stared at the paper in her hand.

"Where he is staying?" Alice asked. "We could send someone after him."

Phoebe frowned and shook her head. "He didn't say."

"And there are dozens of taverns; he might be in any one of them," Edmund added. "Who is the letter addressed to?"

Phoebe showed him the name. He took it from her hand and studied the name.

"I know who that is. In fact, I will be going near his home tomorrow. Let me take it with me and deliver it myself."

"That's a good plan, Edmund," Alice exclaimed, "if you truly don't mind."

"Not at all." Edmund stuffed the letter into his pocket.

Phoebe hesitated, for she felt sure that sooner or later Nicholas would realize he had misplaced the letter and come looking for it. But she did not know where to find Nicholas either, and it would seem churlish to refuse to let Edmund perform the service he had offered. Besides, she was not used to opposing a scheme approved by Alice.

But later, as she lay awake recalling her conversation with Nicholas, she also remembered George's opinion of Nicholas and his warning. Perhaps, after all, she had been foolish to be so pleased by Nicholas's attention. Perhaps it would be better to stay away when he visited. On the other hand, there was no harm in ordinary politeness. It would have been rude to refuse to carry on a conversation with him. She sighed in the dark. It would be much easier to possess a heart of stone, for then she need never question how she should behave.

❧ *Chapter Three* ☙

"Now these stitches look very nice." Phoebe nodded in approval as she examined the sampler spread out in her lap. "The flowers are very neatly done, and that bird in particular is very clever. Did you make it up on your own?"

"I copied it off of one I saw on your sampler." Sally pointed to the sampler hanging on the parlor wall.

"Did you indeed? I thought it looked familiar. But look here, Sally, some of these x's are crossed over the wrong way. You must always cross over from right to left on top, or the stitches won't have a smooth appearance."

Sally's face fell. "Do I have to take all those letters out and do them again?"

Phoebe frowned, glancing from the sampler to her sister's gloomy face. "The stitches up here don't look so bad. Mother might make you do them again, but for now just pull out these few letters and start here."

Sally sighed and took the sampler back. Phoebe thought her sister looked unduly distressed. "Don't worry. You can fix all that in fifteen minutes."

"I know." Sally hesitated, then glanced up at her older sister anxiously. "Phoebe, there is something I need to talk to you about."

"Oh? What is it?"

"Something bad has happened and I don't know what to do about it, and I'm afraid to tell Mother." Sally twisted her hands in her lap, biting her lip, her eyes batting. "You see, Peggy's grandmother gave her a little flute for her birthday, and when Peggy saw how much I liked it, she told me I could take it home with me for a few days. But Kit found it and played with it, and it broke. I'm afraid to tell Mother, because she will say I shouldn't have borrowed Peggy's toy, and when Peggy's mother finds out, she will likely give her a whipping."

Phoebe privately thought it rather hard to whip a child for a simple accident, but did not doubt the likelihood of it.

"Peggy should have asked her mother before she lent you her toy, I suppose," Phoebe admitted. "But perhaps we can try to improve the situation. I will look at the flute and see if it is past mending, and if it is, we can try to buy a new one to replace it. Perhaps Peggy's mother will be less angry if we try to make amends."

Sally's face brightened. "Will you do that, Phoebe? And do I need to tell Mother?"

Phoebe puckered her brow. "I suppose you must."

Sally sighed, but she did seem much relieved, and scampered up the stairs to find the broken flute. Just then Phoebe heard a knock on the door and went to answer it.

Nicholas stood on the step.

Her heart leaped, for she had not seen him in several weeks, since the night he and Edmund had both come calling. She hoped her pleasure was not too obvious, but would not have wagered on it, for she was aware of her own transparency. "Come in," she greeted him, smiling.

Nicholas stepped into the passage, glancing into the open doorways, for the house was remarkably quiet. "Is everyone else away from home?"

He was thinking of Alice, of course. "My mother took Alice and the boys to my uncle's farm to help with the harvesting," she explained. "My father is working in his shop, and I am here with Sally."

"Then perhaps you cannot leave," he said. "I have some errands to run in town, and I thought you might like to come along with me, see the fair and have some supper somewhere. But perhaps today is an inconvenient time."

Had it been the most impossible time in the world, Phoebe would have found a way somehow. Supper for her father and sister was a minor obstacle under the circumstances. "I need a few minutes to get ready," she assured him, "if you are not in too great a hurry."

She ran into the pantry, hunting right and left for something to set out for supper. The lettuce and cucumbers she had just picked from the garden that morning would do, along with the fresh-baked bread and butter. And there was a half of a cherry pie that would make three adequate slices. She would give her father the last piece of shad left from dinner, and persuade Sally to do without. Sally did not care for shad much anyway.

She hurried into the kitchen, dropping the food on the table and fetching plates and spoons. She carried the plate of fish to the fire and set it in a pan to warm. Martha, the housemaid, watched her racing in astonishment.

"I'm walking out with Nicholas Teasdale," she explained, pausing to catch her breath. "The fish is for my father. Just serve the supper when he comes in from the shop. And oh, Martha, please keep an eye on Sally for me, can you? She is working on her sampler and won't be any trouble. Thank you *so* much."

Martha shrugged and turned back to her scrubbing. Phoebe ran up the stairs to the bedroom she shared with her sisters.

She stripped off her soiled apron and her worn waistcoat, then slid into a fresh, clean flowered muslin gown, one with blue ribbons around the neck and sleeves. She pulled off her mobcap, re-pinned her hair, and replaced it with a pinner cap trimmed in lace. Her petticoat, she decided, was clean enough; she did not need hoops for such a casual outing as this, but at least she was wearing her corsets. After a moment of hesitation she wrapped a blue kerchief around her neck and into the low square neckline of her gown, for modesty's sake. Then she picked up her mirror.

Her heart-shaped face looked back at her, very tanned from the summer sun, but her cheeks were flushed a becoming rose, and the blue of the kerchief brought out the sparkling blue of her eyes. Overall, she decided, she looked quite well. Not as fair as Alice, perhaps, but that couldn't be helped. Certainly much more elegant than on the day in July when he had tripped over her at the State House. She picked up her handkerchief and skipped down the stairs.

"All right, I'm ready," she called.

He smiled to himself at the sight of her, and she wondered if he had heard her mad racing around the house. Her cheeks flushed a deeper pink, and with all the dignity she could muster took the arm he offered her. For the rest of the day she was determined to be proper and lady-like and well-behaved.

It was late August, but the weather was cooler than it usually was during the heat of the summer. The sky reflected a clear azure without the heavy whiteness of humidity, and a brisk breeze fanned their faces. They walked toward Market Street, where the fair had come to town, and as they walked, Phoebe asked Nicholas for news of the army.

"I haven't heard of any battles yet," she remarked, thinking of George.

"Not yet," Nicholas agreed, "but 'twill be any day now. The British are building up on Staten Island, and a new fleet arrived this past week with some eight thousand Hessians."

"Hessians!" Phoebe turned to look up at him. "Who are the Hessians?"

"Why, they're mercenaries, of course," Nicholas returned, looking amused. "King George bought them from some prince in Germany. You don't think he would kill off his own soldiers when for a few pence he can kill off the Germans instead."

Phoebe, mystified by the craft of war, shook her head at the idea.

"He certainly respects the Hessians more than he does our army," Nicholas added. "Would you believe, Lord Howe tried to send a letter to General Washington, but refused to call him General, addressing the letter simply 'George Washington, Esquire, etc.' And Howe's adjutant tried to convince Washington to accept the letter by arguing that the 'et cetera' represented all his titles. Do you believe it?" Nicholas chuckled at the memory.

Phoebe stepped over a broken section of cobblestones. "What did Washington do?"

"He refused it, of course. He told the adjutant to deliver it at the end of the war to his estate in Virginia, because that's where 'George Washington, Esquire,' lives."

"Good for him!" Phoebe exclaimed warmly. "That will teach Lord Howe to show him proper respect. But Nicholas, I heard a rumor once about a plot to kill General Washington. Was there any truth to it?"

"Aye, they arrested a dozen or so conspirators, and hanged one of them after a court martial. They even arrested the mayor of New York, who is a Tory, but haven't hanged him, at least not yet."

Phoebe almost stumbled as she looked at him in horror. "The mayor! George told me that New York is full of Tories, but I had no idea. Poor Mr. Washington, he must have no idea whom he can trust."

"There are Tories everywhere, and no one knows whom to trust." His tone matched his grave expression, and then he grinned. He lowered his voice. "There is another part to this story most people don't know; I am only privy to it because of my position. One of the conspirators claimed he actually shared a mistress with Washington, and this woman stole military secrets from Washington and delivered them to the Tories."

"How dreadful!" Phoebe exclaimed, unsure whether to be more shocked that Washington would have a mistress or that the woman would plot to kill him. Did men in high places always behave in such ways?

Nicholas took Phoebe's arm to direct her around a young mother in their path who was trying to round up her four small children. "For my part, I don't completely believe such a story. General Washington may have known this woman, but I can't believe he would be such a ninny as to let her get her hands on military secrets. More likely to my thinking is that she invented the secrets to lend herself importance with her fellow conspirators."

By now they had reached the center of the fair and were distracted from their conversation by the rows and rows of little booths and the sellers hawking their wares. A fiddler approached Nicholas and Phoebe and played them a lively tune, and Nicholas tossed him half a shilling for his effort, which Phoebe, fresh from her mother's frugal influence, considered both generous and extravagant. Nicholas, dressed in his officer's uniform, had the appearance of a gentleman, and Phoebe was conscious of the glances of envy, admiration, and deference with which the more common people drew aside for them.

"Perhaps I can find a new little flute for Sally," she said to Nicholas, and told him the story of the broken gift.

Nicholas chuckled. "And you are assisting your little sister in this deception?" he asked in a tone of mock reproach.

"'Tisn't deception," Phoebe insisted. "We will tell my mother and Peggy's too, but I thought it would help if we could replace the broken one."

She found a little flute she hoped would be adequate, and while she was making her purchase noticed that Nicholas had wandered away and was engaged in conversation with a man in the crowd, a tall hawk-nosed man with bushy black locks that hung over his shoulders. She saw him slip the man a piece of paper before he turned to rejoin her.

They continued examining the stalls, laughing over some items and exclaiming over others. Nicholas bought Phoebe a pretty painted silk fan she admired, and tried to buy her a pearl bracelet, which she refused with difficulty. It was too expensive, and her mother would never approve such a gift from a young man. They ended up at a stall that sold confections, where a skinny little girl in a ragged petticoat stood gazing at the sweets. Nicholas smiled and bought her a piece of rock candy, and then a box of marzipan for Phoebe.

"It will ruin our supper," Phoebe said when he urged her to try a piece.

"Nonsense, I'm still hungry enough to eat a horse. Come, Phoebe, enjoy yourself; your mother isn't here to scold you now."

So she took the offered piece, and because the candy was sweet and the weather was beautiful, because she felt pretty and happy and her escort was lively and the handsomest one at the fair, she wanted to sing. As they strolled along she began one of the hymns from the Methodist service.

Come we that love the Lord, and let our joys be known.
Join in our song with sweet accord and thus surround the throne.
Let those refuse to sing who never knew our God,
But children of the heavenly King should speak their joys abroad.

Nicholas listened to her first song in silence, but when she began the second song he asked, "Are those church hymns? I've never heard them before. They're unlike the hymns at the church where I was raised."

34

"That one was written by Mr. Charles Wesley. He and his brother started the Methodist societies where my family and I attend."

Nicholas studied her for a moment with a thoughtful expression. "Are you as devout as the rest of your family, Phoebe?"

"I hope so," she said earnestly. "I try to be, but I feel like I never measure up."

"Measure up according to whom?"

"I don't know." She considered for a moment as they walked past the next few stalls. "My mother perhaps, or my sister, or God."

"And do God and your mother always agree?"

"I don't know." She tried to laugh off the strange question. "My mother probably thinks so, and I'm sure my sister does."

"You need to stop worrying so much what your family thinks."

Phoebe glanced at him, startled by such heresy. Hadn't Rhoda said the same thing? It still seemed wrong to her. "But I should worry what God thinks, shouldn't I?"

"Perhaps." He shrugged and grinned. "For my own part, I've concluded that God and my father are both impossible to please, and I gave up trying years ago."

Phoebe turned to study his face, troubled by his words, but he laughed and squeezed her arm then as if the whole were just a good-natured joke, and changed the subject.

"Are you hungry? I know a clean little tavern with decent food that's not too far from here. What do you say?"

"That would be lovely." Phoebe found herself relieved to leave the disturbing topic behind. A moment later he was ushering her into a small tavern where they were seated for supper.

It was neither the most elegant nor the most disreputable of the multitude of such establishments in the city, Phoebe saw as she examined their surroundings. The room where they were seated was dark and smoky, with the aroma of ale and codfish heavy in the air. The other patrons wore the garb of common folk, but the place was clean and quiet with no evidence of drunkenness. Nicholas ordered a syllabub and Phoebe, who had acquired the Methodist disapproval of strong drink, an aversion by no means shared by the majority of her countrymen, asked for coffee.

"It has taken me a long time to develop a taste for this," she admitted as she sipped her cup. "I actually like tea much better, but I feel so unpatriotic drinking it now."

"You are a devoted little Rebel, aren't you? Sneaking away from home to hear the Declaration, and shunning tea! But do you think you could be wooed away by some handsome redcoat?"

"I can't imagine it," Phoebe answered seriously. "I know there are many good British soldiers, but I would feel like such a traitor if I fell in love with one."

"I'm so heartened by your loyalty." Nicholas's eyes laughed as he spoke. "I need to tell my fellow soldiers that there are a few true female patriots who can't be seduced by money and power. We don't find many such women in New York, you know." He leaned back in his seat, a pucker appearing between his brows. "Does your sister share your patriotic fervor?"

Phoebe dropped her eyes and tried not to react to the mention of Alice. She had almost succeeded in forgetting about her sister today, and had dared to hope that he had forgotten as well. "Alice is not interested in politics," she said evenly.

"So she would have no objection to a Tory lover." Nicholas twirled his spoon in his fingers. "That fellow who is courting her—Edward? Where does he stand in this conflict?"

Phoebe was surprised by the question. "Edmund? I don't actually know. I've always assumed that he was a Whig, but I've never really heard him discuss the matter."

"I'm sure he is a good Methodist." Phoebe could not tell if Nicholas was mocking. "Alice surely would not have anyone else."

"He does attend the Methodist service," Phoebe admitted, uncomfortable with the whole topic. But then Nicholas grinned at her, and she wondered if he actually cared about Alice or was simply making conversation.

"I'm counting on you to convert them to our cause, Phoebe. You turn them both into good Rebels, and perhaps I'll even join a Methodist society."

She laughed to hide her embarrassment and was relieved when the servant appeared with their suppers. Nicholas dug into his beefsteak with gusto, and while they ate he regaled her with stories of army life, including interesting tidbits about some of the generals and statesmen whose names she had often heard but whom she had never met.

When their meal was finished, Nicholas and Phoebe rose to leave. Nicholas, digging in his pocket for coins, stepped to the side just as a servant at the table behind him stepped backwards, and the two collided. The platter she was carrying tilted and a glass jug slipped and crashed on the wooden floor.

Heads turned all over the room to see the commotion, and the girl dropped onto the floor to try to collect the pieces. Nicholas swore lightly under his breath, glancing at Phoebe with a guilty expression.

"Are you wet?" She examined his uniform with concern.

Nicholas shrugged. "Not very. I think the jug was mostly empty."

They both stepped back as the tavern keeper rushed into the scene, blasting the servant girl with threats and a shaking.

"Worthless wench," he raged, adding a kick at the huddled figure for good measure. "I'll never let you handle my good glassware again!" He turned to Nicholas, eying his uniform warily. "My profuse apologies, sir. That girl is very clumsy."

"'Twas my fault entirely." Nicholas reached into his pocket for a coin to sweeten the man's mood. The servant peeked up at him, and Phoebe saw Nicholas give her a wink. "Perhaps you could stick with pewter," he added to the owner. "It doesn't shatter as easily."

He took Phoebe by the arm and guided her to the door.

"I'm glad you defended that girl," she said as soon as they were out of hearing. "He seems like a most unpleasant master."

Nicholas shrugged. "Accidents happen, and he couldn't beat me as easily as her."

He glanced left and right up the street; she had the feeling he had something else on his mind. "Can you wait here just a moment, Phoebe? I'll be back quickly."

He slipped into the alley that ran along the side of the tavern. Phoebe waited a few minutes and then, curious, peeked into the alley to see if he had disappeared. She saw him lift the lid of a crate in the alley and stuff something white into his pocket.

How odd, she reflected. *To be sure he is a courier, but he seems to pick up letters in the strangest places.* First the man in the crowd at the fair, and now this. Clearly he had not wanted Phoebe to see what he was doing. She drew back and tried to seem oblivious when he came out of the alley.

"I'm ready now." He gave her a cheerful smile. "Listen, Phoebe, there's a pretty little walkway down by the river, and I thought we might take a turn in it before we go home."

Phoebe hesitated, for she knew it would be wiser for her to be home before her mother returned. She glanced at the sun sinking on the horizon. Surely with all the work at her uncle's, her mother would not be home before dark. Who knew when she would spend another such lovely day, or when she would even see Nicholas again? "If we don't tarry long," she smiled up at him.

He smiled back at her and she felt her heart catch at the look on his face. The air had cooled from the heat of the afternoon, and as they strolled along the river the breeze carried the scent of muddy water and dried the sweat on their faces. Nicholas became quieter and held her hand as they walked together. They passed sailors along the landing, a cluster of little girls playing scotch-hoppers, and a pair of boys fishing in the river.

Today has been the most perfect day, Phoebe thought. *If only it would never end.*

Nicholas led her into a little sheltered path and to a small clearing surrounded by shrubbery. He removed his coat and spread it on the grass. "Let's watch the stars come out," he suggested with a smile.

Her heart racing oddly, Phoebe settled beside him and spread her petticoat down over her feet. Nicholas's sleeve just rested against her own. They stared up at the sky for a moment in silence.

"I see the first star!" Her voice came out barely above a whisper.

Nicholas turned his head to watch her face. "Are you going to make a wish?"

"I—I don't know," she whispered. "What should I wish for?"

"I know what I would wish," Nicholas said.

Phoebe turned toward him, met his gaze, and lowered her own in confusion. Her heart was hammering so loudly she could hear it. She felt one of his arms go around her back, and then he drew her against him and kissed her.

It was her first real kiss, she exulted. The kiss from Rhoda's brother under the mistletoe last Christmas didn't really count, and neither did the kiss on the cheek she had received when she was sixteen. And it was the most perfect kiss imaginable, warm and sweet and delicious, and from the one man in the world whom she most wanted to kiss.

Nicholas kissed her once, and then a second time, and then a third. Through the pounding of her heart and the swirling confusion of her emotions, it suddenly dawned on her that he had no intention of stopping after a few kisses. Having never found herself in such a situation before, Phoebe had no idea how to react. She felt him pull away the kerchief she had tucked into her bodice and kiss her on the neck.

Startled, she pulled back. "Nicholas, what—what are you doing?"

He tried to draw her close again. "Just enjoying the evening with you, Phoebe."

"Enjoying the evening!" she spluttered.

She glanced around at their surroundings. The sun had long since vanished and the greenery around them was fading to gray in the dusk. There was no one in sight, only, far away, the piping voices of the children and the rough ones of the sailors. She was suddenly aware of the impropriety of being here alone with him after dark.

She pulled out of his arms, groped for where her cap had fallen in the grass, and adjusted the neckline of her bodice. Fortunately all her buttons were still fastened. She wet her lips and swallowed.

"I don't know if this is your idea of enjoying the evening," she said, trying to keep the tremble out of her voice, "but 'tisn't mine. Do you behave this way with every girl you meet?"

"What do you mean?" He drew back and folded his arms, glaring at her, and Phoebe couldn't tell if he were more annoyed or indignant.

"We're not betrothed, we're not even courting." Suddenly she remembered that she was just a stand-in for her sister. If Alice had been at home today instead of with her mother, Nicholas no doubt would have invited her instead. "You—you aren't even interested in me, you're interested in Alice!"

"Who—who told you that?" Nicholas stammered.

Phoebe searched his face, hunting for a clue to his emotions. "Well, it is obvious. She's the one you talk to all the time—you wouldn't even have asked me here today except that she was away from home."

Nicholas opened his mouth to protest again, then flushed and remained silent. A well of silence opened between them. Nicholas rose to his feet.

"You are right." His tone was cool. "I was sporting with you, and that was not gentlemanly of me. I apologize, Phoebe."

He held out his hand to help her up, but she scrambled to her feet without his assistance. "You were trying to seduce me," she said stiffly.

At that he suddenly broke into laughter. "Just like Mr. B! Poor Pamela! Next I was planning to carry you off to my country estate and hold you prisoner!"

Phoebe bit her lip, torn between anger and mortification. The sickness of disappointment churned in her stomach and she felt tears sting her eyes, which she would die rather than let him see. Nicholas was clearly accustomed to kissing girls. It meant nothing to him. He'd probably felt no more genuine attachment for any of them than he did for Phoebe. How could she have been so foolish? She turned and started back down the path toward home.

He fell into step beside her and after a moment of silence squeezed her arm. "Don't be so angry with me, Phoebe." His tone was both penitent and cajoling. "'Twas only a kiss, after all."

No thanks to you, Phoebe thought. *The Lord only knows what you really wanted.* But she did not trust herself to speak, to expose her indignation to his levity or her disappointment to his pity.

They walked mostly in silence until they reached the Fuller home. "I am leaving tomorrow for New York," Nicholas told her as they approached the door.

"I wish you a very safe journey," Phoebe returned. He bowed once, turned, and started down the walk, and Phoebe opened the door to her home and went in.

ℰ𝒪 *Chapter Four* ℭ𝔰

The war, which had simmered along to no great effect for months, suddenly boiled over at the end of August. Word trickled down to Philadelphia of a battle fought on Brooklyn Heights, and although reports at first were contradictory and confusing, it soon became clear that Washington's army had been decimated, with over a thousand men captured and nearly as many killed or wounded. The only good news for the Rebel cause seemed to be that Howe had allowed the Continental army to escape back across the harbor into New York, when he might easily have crushed it.

Sarah Fuller was frantic for news of George, and the whole family seemed to hold its collective breath for two weeks until they received a letter which assured them that, although his cause might be crippled, George himself was alive and well. But once they were reassured on that point, there seemed little else to cheer them. The battle was George's first real combat, and Phoebe could sense that her brother was badly shaken by the experience.

"The mercenary Hessians are especially dreadful warriors, and made us feel their brutality," he wrote. "I have heard tales from different sources, that they bayoneted fleeing Yankees in the back, that they slaughtered those who were trying to surrender, and in one horrible case pinned a young boy to a tree with a bayonet, leaving him to writhe there in agony for hours. You can imagine how such reports intensify our dread of battle."

The women of the family could certainly imagine it, and their own horror was multiplied when other rumors of the Hessians reached them. The mercenaries had looted and plundered the homes of civilians in Brooklyn, using excrement to defile the houses in order to make them uninhabitable. Women were raped in their own homes; old people were murdered.

How many of these rumors were actually true they had no way of knowing, but the loathsomeness of the tales convinced them that if only a portion were legitimate, the Hessians must be terrifying indeed. The poor women of New York! And only Washington's army stood between the enemy and Philadelphia! The British at least were their countrymen, bound by ties of blood and history, however misguided and estranged. But the Hessians!

"You see how dreadful King George is," Rhoda remarked in an undertone as she and Phoebe sat together in the Fuller kitchen soon afterward, peeling apples for pies that Pheobe's mother wanted to bake. "He claims we are his subjects, his own countrymen, but here he's sent this brutal army of savages to murder and rape and plunder us all. That shows what a tyrant he is. He cares nothing about the colonists, he just wants to subdue us, and he'll stop at nothing."

Phoebe shuddered. "It does seem that way. Even Alice was shocked by the stories about the Hessians. She's never cared about taxes or representative government or anything of that sort. But these stories have upset her and my mother too. How do the Hessians even know who is loyal to the crown and who is a rebel? That's what my mother wonders about. We hear everyone is treated the same, even if they've stayed loyal all along."

Rhoda nodded, a triumphant flash in her eyes. "'Tis true! If the King really saw us as true Englishmen, do you think he would treat us this way? Would he bring the Hessians into England to behave this way? That's what my father says. So now all the loyalists who've defended the King see what he really thinks of us all. Maybe it will open their eyes to the truth."

"It will have one effect or the other: turn them against the King, or frighten them into loyalty. I don't know which." If Phoebe were living in New Jersey, just across the Delaware River from Philadelphia, which way would she turn? Her sympathies lay with the rebels, even though she still debated within herself whether they had the right to overthrow their legal historic rulers. When the rulers committed such atrocities, was it acceptable to "institute new government," as the Declaration insisted? Did governments really "derive their just powers from the consent of the governed," and could the governed therefore overthrow them at will? Of course God put governments in power, but maybe that didn't preclude people from choosing new rulers if it would "effect their safety and happiness." Or was that reasoning wrong? She wished she knew for sure.

Aloud she said, "My mother says that it's our duty to obey the government, and so it must be wrong to overthrow the king."

Rhoda glanced around the kitchen, keeping her voice low. "My father was talking to his friends about that very subject just last night. And one of them was telling us about the revolution that they had in England just about a hundred years ago—I think it was called the Glorious Revolution. I don't think I knew about it before. But Mr. Norton was saying that the British overthrew the king then, but fortunately they didn't have to go to war to do it. That's why they called it the Glorious Revolution, because nobody died. They got rid of James the Second and put William and Mary in his place, and they decided—I wish I could remember exactly how he explained it—but that's when they decided that the king could only rule "by the consent of the people" or something like that. So if they can overthrow the king whenever they want, why can't we do the same?" Rhoda gave her a triumphant look.

Phoebe nodded slowly. "I think I remember hearing about the Glorious Revolution, but I never understood it all."

"Well, it seems hypocritical to tell us that we're obligated to be loyal to King George after they got rid of King James because they didn't like his rule. We're standing up for our rights the same way they did back then. Do you see what I mean?"

"Yes, that makes sense. We shouldn't have to accept a ruler we don't like."

But even if she were completely convinced of the ethicality of this action, would she have the moral courage to stand up for her beliefs in the face of death? To behave as George and Nicholas were doing? Or would she turn coward and sign the loyalty oath as so many others colonists were doing?

Phoebe could not hear the news of the battle of Brooklyn Heights without reflecting that Nicholas had also been involved, but she tried to dismiss the thought as quickly as possible. The memory of their last meeting made her wince inside with chagrin and mortification. Her brother had tried to warn her that Nicholas did not have a reputation for the highest morals, and his own comments to her had certainly indicated he did not share her religious convictions, but she had allowed her attraction for him to override her good judgment. And then she had compounded her folly by displaying her feelings to him and imagining they might be reciprocated. What a fool she had been!

Just once, the next day, she had been tempted to confide in Alice about the experience, but she knew her sister well enough to predict her response, almost to the exact words. "Really, Phoebe, what were you thinking to go off alone with a man you barely knew, who had never even asked Papa for permission to court you? You should have known he had no honorable intentions. Next time, don't be such a ninny." So Phoebe had prudently held her tongue and spared herself the lecture.

How had George described her during their last conversation? *Soft and sentimental and persuadable.* Nicholas surely held the same opinion, possibly adding *very silly* to the list, but then, she did not have a very high opinion of him now, either. She would probably never see him again, and that was a relief. Her chief comfort was that no real harm had been done, and her insight into Nicholas's character had gone far to crush her schoolgirl infatuation. Next time she would be more cautious, more prudent.

The month of September passed with news of more battles trickling down from the north. Lord Howe successfully crossed the East River and occupied the city, welcomed by the swarms of Tories in New York. Washington's struggling army was pushed farther north. Phoebe heard names that meant little to her: Kip's Bay, Harlem Heights, Montressor's Island. She prayed for George and tried not to think about Nicholas and overall sensed that they had little to feel encouraged about.

One evening when Edmund was visiting and the family gathered in the parlor, Edmund introduced the topic of the war. Phoebe had never heard him speak on the subject before and had always assumed that he, like Alice, had no political persuasions at all.

"I hear the redcoats are pushing the Rebels all around New York," he remarked, sipping the noggin of cider Phoebe had brought him. "As soon as Washington settles in one place, Howe comes along and kicks him out. The next thing we know Washington and his army will be knocking on doors here in Philadelphia, begging for protection."

His tone of levity filled Phoebe with surprise and indignation. She glanced around the circle of her family, waiting for someone to speak. Her mother was scolding Kit for ripping his new breeches and appeared not to have heard the remark. Alice was sewing peacefully. Her father looked up from the Bible in his lap and gave Edmund a troubled look, but said nothing.

"Washington will never be pushed this far." Phoebe jabbed her needle through the petticoat she was embroidering and pricked her finger on the other side. She put her hand to her mouth to keep the drop of blood from staining the petticoat.

Edmund shrugged. "Time will tell. Up till now the Rebels have been marching around and making a lot of noise, playing soldier. Now they know what it's like to face a real army."

"Poor George." Alice shook her head over the shirt in her lap. "What a terrible time he must be having. I hope he hasn't made a dreadful mistake, joining the army."

Edmund nodded. "Your brother is a romantic. I'm sure going off to war seemed very exciting when he was safely at home. Now he's learning what it's really like."

"He's fighting for a cause he believes in." Phoebe had never argued with Edmund before, and could feel her heartbeat quicken, but someone had to stand up for George and the cause. What was wrong with her family? "Nobody said it would be easy or pleasant, but what if everyone wanted to stay home and be comfortable? Who would fight for freedom?"

"Freedom!" Edmund's voice was heavy with contempt and indignation. "Do you think if Congress and Washington win this war you will be freer than you are under King George? Do you think Congress won't tax their subjects into the ground to pay for this war and all the other wars they'll need to fight to keep their 'freedom'? That's how this whole thing got started, you know. We fought a war right here in America to get rid of the French, and someone had to pay for it. That's why the King taxed us. The colonists here want the protection of British troops but don't want to pay for it."

Phoebe tried to remember what he was talking about. She had been born during the French and Indian War but barely remembered it. It seemed so long ago, irrelevant. She had never been to college, of course; she knew less about history than Edmund and would never be able to win an argument on those grounds.

"We don't want the protection of British troops." She felt sure of that point. "Look at the way they treated the people of Boston. Look at how the King has sent the Hessians against us. That's not how a good king should treat his subjects. If we were treated as equal to the people of England maybe it would be different, but we're treated like slaves and children. We just want the British to leave us to rule ourselves."

Edmund's lips compressed into a thin line and a hard, impatient note crept into his voice. "You've been listening to rhetoric from your rebel friends, Phoebe. You don't understand the way the world really works, what it takes for a country to be safe and secure. If these American colonists succeed in getting rid of King George the Third, they'll end up with another King George, a farmer from Virginia. We'll see if they enjoy his treatment more."

"George Washington will never become king!" Phoebe spluttered. "Do you think he's doing this for his own power? Is that what you believe?"

"All generals want power. Look at Cromwell. He succeeded in deposing the King of England, and then he became as ruthless a dictator as any king ever was. Twenty years later the English people were begging the royal family to take the throne again. I wouldn't be surprised if the colonists do the same."

Phoebe's breath was nearly taken away by his cool audacity. She glanced around the circle of her family to see their reaction. Her mother had finished with Kit and now was listening to Edmund. She nodded as he finished speaking.

"There is a great deal of truth to what you say, Edmund. One ruler is as good as another in my opinion. I don't understand why everyone can't just try to get along."

Phoebe opened her mouth to speak again, trying to remember what

Rhoda had told her about the Glorious Revolution, but she knew she didn't understand the issues well and would sound ignorant and benighted next to Edmund's superior education. She caught Alice's warning glare and fell silent. Her father changed the subject, asking Edmund about his mother's health, and her mother offered him a recipe to cure a persistent fever. But when Alice and Phoebe were preparing for bed that night Alice broached the subject again.

"Don't try to argue politics with Edmund, Phoebe. You don't know as much about it as he does, and it makes you sound foolish. When men talk about things like that you should just pretend to agree, even if you don't."

Phoebe slid out of her petticoats and unhooked her corsets with a glance at her sister's perfect figure. "I've never heard him say those things before," she began slowly. "Do you think Edmund is a Tory, Alice?"

"Oh, nonsense." Alice shook her head so that her loose, shimmering gold hair swung across her shoulders. "I don't think Edmund really cares about the subject at all. He's never discussed it with me either, until tonight."

"He certainly sounded like a Tory to me," Phoebe persisted. "Saying that the King has a right to tax us and that if we win independence, we'll be begging the King to take us back."

"Well, those are his opinions." Alice began to braid her hair with quick fingers. "You don't have to label everyone Tory and Whig, as if we all have to take sides."

Phoebe climbed into bed without speaking. It was hard for her to imagine how anyone could remain neutral in such a conflict. But she knew Alice would disagree.

"And another thing." Alice sat on the side of the bed and looked down at Phoebe before climbing under the covers. "Don't go telling your political friends, the Kirbys, or other people either, that Edmund is a Tory. People are so intolerant with this war going on, especially now that it's going badly for the rebels. I don't want Edmund to be persecuted because of some opinion he voiced in the privacy of our own family. Do you understand?"

Phoebe nodded. She didn't want to get Edmund into trouble, even if he was completely wrong about this war. She had heard of Tories being tarred and feathered and mistreated in other ways. Perhaps that sort of violence was equally wrong. She hoped Edmund would be careful whom he voiced his opinions to. Perhaps the next time he expressed his ideas about Washington and Cromwell and the French and Indian War, he would be conversing with someone more knowledgeable and persuasive than Phoebe, someone who could win him over to the cause. She hoped so, for his sake and for Alice's.

The conversation replayed in her mind over the next few days and troubled her. Maybe Edmund was right when he said kings had to use taxes to pay for wars. That certainly made sense—she had never thought about how wars were funded. Maybe George Washington really did want to become a dictator and would be just like Cromwell. How could she know? If only she could talk to someone about her concerns, perhaps she would feel better about them. If only George were home—if only she could talk to Nicholas! But that was a foolish thought. Nicholas was gone from her life, and it was wrong to even want him to return. She had been so cold at their parting that she felt sure he would not show his face at the Fuller house again.

A few nights later Rhoda invited her to sup with the Kirby family. When the family gathered around the table she found that Mr. Kirby's friend Mr. Jones, another member of the Associators, was also joining them. In this company there was no ambivalence about the war, no disagreement about the justness of the cause. The only source of tension was a fear of defeat, especially after the disaster on Brooklyn Heights. Listening as the two men discussed war strategy, Phoebe longed to share Edmund's views and seek reassurance from the more enlightened, but her promise to her sister prevented her.

"The colonial generals are so inexperienced," she heard Mr. Kirby say. "The men are raw, of course, but the generals are worse. Washington himself has very little experience compared with the British generals. 'Tis an enormous problem. We need leadership in this war to turn the situation around. Washington can't seem to win a battle."

Mr. Jones nodded, frowning. "Washington lost one of his few good generals when Lord Stirling was captured, but fortunately—"

"Lord Stirling!" Phoebe exclaimed, before she could catch herself from interrupting. "When was *he* captured?"

48

The two men turned to her, surprised by her outburst.

"Lord Stirling and his men were caught in a very bad spot on Brooklyn Heights, trying to hold open the road for the army's retreat," Mr. Jones explained gravely. "They were trapped between the British and the Hessians; many of them were slaughtered, and the rest were taken prisoner."

Phoebe blanched in horror as she recalled George's stories of the Hessians. "Merciful heavens!"

Mrs. Kirby gave her a sympathetic look from the other end of the table. "Are you thinking of your brother, Phoebe?"

"Nay," Phoebe managed, "we have heard from George, so we know he survived, but—" she broke off.

"Lord Stirling will be exchanged," Mr. Jones added, "which is fortunate for Washington. He needs all the good officers he can find."

Phoebe tried to frame the question in her mind. "Will *all* the officers be exchanged?"

The men glanced at each other, and Mr. Jones spread his hands. "It depends on the agreement with the British. They exchange officers of equal rank. Sadly, we are more desperate for men than the enemy is."

The conversation moved on at that point, but Phoebe heard none of it, for her mind was riveted on the calamity that had befallen Lord Stirling's men. The words continued to haunt her, playing round and round in her mind over the next days. *Many of them were slaughtered, and the rest were taken prisoner.* Maybe Nicholas was the Yankee who had been pinned to a tree with a bayonet and left to writhe in agony for hours. Nay, George had described him as a boy. Either way, he might very easily be lying dead now, or rotting on a stinking British prison ship, which was in itself nearly a death sentence. Or he might have been wounded; he might have lost an arm, or a leg, or an eye. How would Nicholas manage to live, being so horribly maimed?

Of course, Nicholas's fate was nothing to her. He had admitted that he was only sporting with her, and it was only sensible for her to learn to match his indifference with her own. Still, they had been friends of a sort; wasn't it natural for her to care about his ultimate fate? To care if he were alive or dead?

If George were to die, the family would probably learn of it eventually from his commander or a fellow soldier. But if Nicholas were to die, they would likely never hear at all. They had no mutual friends, and the Fuller family had had no contact with the Teasdale family in several years. It would never occur to anyone who knew Nicholas that any of the Fullers would want to be told of his death.

For a moment Phoebe considered asking Mr. Kirby for information about him. But Mr. Kirby was not acquainted with Nicholas and might not know how to find out, and the awkwardness of such a request deterred her. On the other hand, if she were to write to Lavinia—she wouldn't actually need to ask about Nicholas, but if he had been killed or captured, and Lavinia answered her letter, she would certainly mention it, wouldn't she?

For several days she pondered the idea, dismissing it several times, only to have it recur an hour later. Writing to Lavinia seemed like such an innocent, natural thing to do. No one would read any ulterior motive into a letter—would they? After all, she didn't want to actually *see* Nicholas, only to know if he was alive and well. And her friendship with Lavinia had always been a source of pleasure to them both. What could be wrong with it?

One afternoon as all these doubts and questions revolved through her mind, she sat down at her father's desk and, on an impulse, grabbed a sheet of paper and a quill. She prepared her materials, uncertain all the while whether she actually intended to use them, then dipped the tip into the inkwell.

My dear Lavinia,

It has been so many years since I have heard from you, and I hope you will pardon my presumption in renewing our correspondence after so much time. I do hope this letter finds you and your family in good health. I happened to meet your brother Nicholas here in town one day, and he told me he had left you all well. It was good to hear of you again after so long.

My brother George is serving with Washington's army, and we are all greatly concerned by the news of the most recent battles. We received a letter from him after Brooklyn Heights, but nothing in nearly a month, and my mother in particular is quite anxious. I am certain your family must feel the same anxiety and I hope your brother has come through the fighting safely.

There! she thought, rereading the two paragraphs. *That strikes the right note, just politely concerned. The worst that could happen is Lavinia could mention the letter to Nicholas, and that might give him mischievous thoughts.* For a second she almost crumpled the note until she realized that Lavinia might not see her brother for months. With a war going on, they would surely have more important matters to discuss.

Am I doing a foolish thing, Lord? she prayed silently. *I was foolish before, and I don't want to be so again. Perhaps I should mention the letter to my mother, and if she approves, I will send it.*

She finished the letter with trivial news. She folded it and carried it into the kitchen, where her mother was churning butter and Alice was mixing ingredients for baking bread.

"I've just written to Lavinia Teasdale," she mentioned casually, fetching a cloth to wipe the table where Alice was working. "Do you have any letters to mail?"

"How lovely!" her mother exclaimed. "You two used to be such friends. Be sure to send my greetings to her mother."

Phoebe obediently opened the paper to add a postscript, rereading the first two paragraphs again.

"They are so rich now, they probably have more important friends," Alice remarked. "They might not care to hear from us."

"Nonsense, Alice, Nicholas wasn't so proud when he visited last summer. He was very friendly and obliging."

Aye, Phoebe thought. *Friendly and obliging indeed.*

"True." Alice carefully measured the milk into her bowl. "But for marriage, they would certainly look higher than us."

"Perhaps so." Her mother lifted the bread dough from the bowl and began to knead it. "But no one is thinking of marriage here. Phoebe is Lavinia's old friend, and I think it is very fine that she has written to her."

Alice raised her eyebrows, glancing at her sister, and Phoebe felt the color rise in her cheeks. For a moment she nearly tossed the letter into the fire. But it was already written and her mother approved, so she would send it and then try to put it out of her mind.

ဆ ဢ

Nicholas cantered up to the house where George Washington was lodged and swung down from his mare, Syllabub. At the door he was met by the general's aide and handed him the letter.

"Message from Lord Stirling for General Washington," Nicholas told him. "I was told to wait for a response."

The aide vanished within and Nicholas turned to stroll through the front garden. Heavy clouds were rolling across the sky as a damp wind picked up strength. The hills surrounding White Plains displayed their autumn splendor, crimson and gold and burnt orange, but he knew that soon the colors would fade to brown and vanish in the driving wind. And what would come of the army then? Only October, and already the enlisted men were half-starved and poorly clad and sleeping on the cold damp ground at night. Winter would only intensify their miseries—if, indeed, the army had not disintegrated by winter time.

A fresh-faced, rosy young private who worked in the stables came forward from around the house to see who was calling on the general. Walton was twenty-one and looked younger, barely old enough to shave, Nicholas reflected with amusement, but just two months ago he had obtained leave and married his sixteen-year-old sweetheart. The two men exchanged greetings.

"Have you heard the news?" Nicholas asked him. "Colonel Haslet crossed the Bronx River with a raiding party and caught Robert Rogers and his Tories by surprise. They killed a mess, captured thirty-six men and brought back a pile of muskets as well."

"I was hoping you would say he wiped out Howe's entire army," Walton grinned.

"No such luck. But I'll take any victory we can get right now. We need one badly."

Walton nodded glumly. "We're in for another fight soon, I reckon."

"It looks that way," Nicholas concurred. "Maybe you should take a minute to write to your little lady in the next few days."

Walton's eyes brightened. "I heard from her last week. She is with child! Do you believe it?"

"Congratulations." Nicholas laughed silently. "You must have kept busy during your one week at home."

Walton grinned, embarrassed and proud, then his expression darkened. "I'm mighty glad she has her parents to look out for her right now. I won't be any use to her for a while."

Nicholas reflected that his young friend would scarcely enjoy the pleasures of either marriage or fatherhood anytime soon, and nodded grimly. The aide returned with a response for Lord Stirling, and Nicholas swung up onto Syllabub, waved farewell, and kicked the mare into a trot.

What was it about war and carnage that made young men like Walton rush off into matrimony? He had noticed the same phenomenon repeatedly. Was it a sudden awareness of the shortness of life? The urge to leave progeny behind? A quest for security in a world turned upside down? A yearning for female companionship in an all-male society? Or simply the sudden maturity that came from sacrifice and hardship and daily facing the grim realities of life?

He had faced the same questions about himself. Just six months ago he would have laughed at the notion of settling down with one woman anytime in the foreseeable future. But that was before the newness and excitement of army life had worn down to a monotonous daily struggle for survival. That was before so many of his comrades—most of them younger than himself—had been slaughtered on Brooklyn Heights. Sheer luck that he had made his escape back to Rebel lines before the Hessians closed in. He could just as easily be lying, unrecognized and unburied, in the wood of horror with the hundreds of other corpses, and who would know or care?

Irrelevantly his mind went back to that last carefree day in Philadelphia with Phoebe. It was true that he had first planned to ask Alice, for reasons he could scarcely explain to her sister. But he had been surprised at how much he enjoyed her company that afternoon. She was pretty and fun-loving, curious and warm-hearted, with an innocence he found both amusing and endearing. And she did not bother to hide the fact that she found him attractive. But when he had tried to push his advantage, later in the day in the woods, she had quickly shown her mettle and put him in his place.

Well, that was that. He had almost begun to think of the Fuller house as his second home—his *first* home now—but he hardly dared show his face there again. Phoebe had no doubt told her strict mother and her starchy sister that Nicholas had taken her off into the woods to try to have his way with her. Well, it was his own fault; he should have known better. What a fool!

He tried to shrug the whole incident off as he had many times in the last two months. His father would not approve of the Fuller daughters as marriage material, for they were only apothecary's daughters and would have no fortune apart from a modest marriage settlement. Now that he was the oldest son, he would be expected to improve the family fortunes with an advantageous match. But his mother would approve of Phoebe. Phoebe reminded him of his mother in many ways: her zest for life, her affectionate heart, her piety.

Suddenly he was swept with a wave of homesickness so intense that it was all he could do to keep from turning around and galloping Syllabub straight through the British lines to his home. He wanted to throw himself in his mother's arms and feel her rub his head the way she had when he was a little boy. He wanted to hear Lavinia and Charlotte chatter about their parties and beaux. He wanted to taste Sadie's good cooking, to tease the housemaids, to sleep in his own bed next to the little window where he could feel the breeze blow over him during the summer nights and watch the stars turn in the sky. He even wanted to visit Philip's grave and hear the neighbors remark what a fine, honorable young man his brother had been. But if he went home, his father would think that he was sorry, and he wasn't. If he went home, his father would expect him to apologize, and he couldn't. He was trapped in his self-imposed exile.

With a pain in his chest that hurt when he breathed, he rode Syllabub straight back toward Lord Stirling's camp and his next battle.

☙ Chapter Five ❧

"Another battle!" Sarah dropped the newspaper onto the chair beside her and covered her face with her hands. "White Plains, it says this time. Over six weeks now with no word. How are we ever going to find out if George is alive or dead?"

Alice moved to her mother's side and put her arm around her. Phoebe picked up the discarded newspaper and scanned it. Another defeat for the colonists. Her heart sank. It had been one disaster after another during the last few months.

"How can we trust total strangers to look after our boy?" Sarah went on, wringing her hands. "Would anyone even bother to write to us if he were killed? We might never know!"

"We can't assume that George is dead." Alice covered her mother's agitated hands with her own. "I think we'd hear something if anything were wrong, sooner or later."

"Then why hasn't George written? Why haven't we heard anything? I told him to write once a month, without fail, so we would know. And he always has until now."

Phoebe folded the paper and came to sit on the other side of her mother. "You have to think how difficult it must be for George to write now. The army is constantly moving and in danger. Even if he could get a paper and pen, the letter might be impossible to send, or might get lost and stolen."

Alice nodded. "Aye, I think it would be almost impossible to get a

55

letter to us right now. He'll surely write sooner or later, when he has the opportunity. We just have to be patient."

Sarah wiped her eyes and rose to her feet. "I knew nothing good would come of this. I'll lose my firstborn, and all for what? He could have stayed safely at home and be helping his father in the shop."

"We haven't lost him yet," Alice said gently.

Sarah took a deep breath and marched to the kitchen table. "Come, Phoebe, let's get these pies finished. Edmund might come calling tonight and we need to have something to offer him."

Edmund did come courting that evening, and to their surprise he was accompanied by a friend of his, whom he introduced to the family as Miles Quincy. His friend was a tall, rather heavy young man in his early twenties, with a florid complexion, dark, thinning hair with a receding hairline, and a ponderous manner. He had an unusually deep voice and a tendency to speak in a low, gravelly monotone.

Edmund took his usual seat next to Alice in the parlor and Mr. Quincy seated himself next to Phoebe. He smiled at her and cleared his throat, and after a moment of silence, spoke.

"Good evening, ma'am."

"Good evening." Phoebe tried to think of something else to say to him. Clearly Edmund and Alice expected her to entertain him while they visited together. "Do you live near here, Mr. Quincy?"

He nodded. "I live here in Philadelphia, but I met Edmund up at the College of New Jersey. We were students there together."

"I see." A pause. "What did you study there? Are you a lawyer like Edmund?"

"No, ma'am, I am planning to join the ministry. I'm preparing for my ordination in the Church of England."

Phoebe had great respect for ministers, and her opinion of Miles Quincy climbed several notches. "How very interesting. Do you think you will be given a church here in Philadelphia?"

"I certainly hope so, for my family all live nearby and I would be sorry to leave. My mother is a widow, you see, and I need to take care of my mother. She has poor health, you see, so I need to take care of her."

"That's very good of you." Phoebe nodded in approval.

"I have a sister, but she has a large family and 'tis hard for her to give my mother the attention she needs. She has six children, with another—er, well, another, another to arrive soon." He blushed scarlet and looked so distressed that Phoebe almost felt sorry for him. "Her oldest boy is only eight, no, let me see, he turned nine last week. That's right, he was born the last week of October, nine years ago, so that would mean he turned nine last week. And Abigail is seven, Joshua is six, Aaron four, Simon three, and the baby—I always forget her name— the baby is just over a year old. So you see, my sister is very busy, and can't help my mother as much as she would like."

"I can understand that. She must be terribly busy with so many little ones."

"I have another sister, but she married a man from New York and lives too far away to be much help to my mother. I'm sure my sister would *like* to help, you understand. She feels badly that she lives so far away. The last time she came to visit—it was last spring, before all this war business got underway—she tried to persuade my mother to move up there to New York with her. 'Miles,' she said to me, 'Miles, I would be happy to take Mamma to New York with me, but she is so stubborn, she refuses to budge. She refuses to leave the home she has always lived in. I'm sorry all this care is falling upon you alone.' That is what my sister said to me."

"That was very kind of her, I'm sure."

"Aye, it was kind of her, but my mother can be stubborn like that sometimes. I think, to be honest, my brother-in-law was rather relieved that my mother refused. And I have a younger brother as well. I don't mean to criticize my brother, but he isn't very useful in helping with my mother. He likes to go off with young fellows his own age and only comes home to eat and sleep. That's what I say, only to eat and sleep. So, you see, that's why I'm the one who takes care of my mother."

"'Tis most fortunate for her that she has a good son like you to care for her."

To her amazement he actually blushed again. "Thank you, ma'am, for saying so."

On her left elbow she heard Alice laughing over a story Edmund was telling her. Phoebe bit her lip, trying to suppress her frustration with the situation. Miles Quincy did seem like a nice young man and very devoted to his mother. But after spending a half hour conversing with him she was left with the hope that his sermons were more scintillating than his conversation, or he would leave his congregation sleeping each week. He spoke in great length about other members of his family, whom Phoebe had never met, and his studies in college, and Phoebe nodded politely and smiled and tried to ask intelligent questions. Privately she guessed he had little experience with women and less understanding of how to recommend himself to the opposite sex, and she couldn't help comparing him with Nicholas in that regard. But Nicholas's experience with women was all of the wrong sort, and Mr. Quincy at least seemed like a decent man, so Phoebe tried to be pleasant to him for Edmund's sake.

When the two men rose to leave, Edmund suggested the four of them take a ride the next Sunday afternoon in his new carriage. They would drive to Germantown for tea and cakes, if the weather were agreeable. Phoebe found little pleasure in the prospect, but the other three were enthusiastic about the idea, and she hated to wet-blanket their scheme. So the next Sunday Edmund and Miles arrived at the Fuller house and lifted the two sisters into the carriage.

The actual outing was not much different than she had anticipated. Alice and Edmund spoke mostly to each other, or the men discussed their studies or college companions who were strangers to Phoebe. For a while they talked about the death of one friend from smallpox and the funeral they had both attended. Miles gave his opinion on the proper etiquette for funerals and how he intended to handle them when he was ordained. The conversation moved to Edmund's cousin who was planning to be married. Alice remembered the cousin from a dinner at Edmund's house, but Phoebe had never met him. Then Edmund told Alice about his aunt's reaction to her future daughter-in-law and Alice asked questions while Phoebe and Miles rode side by side in silence.

Phoebe tried to think of something to say to her companion.

"Have you read any interesting books lately?" she asked him.

Alice, overhearing her, laughed.

"Don't imagine that Miles ever reads novels, Phoebe, and you rarely read anything else," she said. "But perhaps he will infect you with his better taste."

Phoebe flushed and fell silent.

"Last month I read a book of sermons by Jonathan Edwards," Miles began. "Have you heard of him?"

Phoebe nodded.

"He was a great preacher here in America. One of the leaders of the Great Awakening. He wasn't ordained in the Church of England, of course, so in that sense I can't claim to agree with him theologically on every point. But he was a great preacher nonetheless. The most famous of his sermons is called 'Sinners in the Hands of an Angry God.' That's the one most people associate with Jonathan Edwards, but I've read another sermon I think I prefer, that is more in my style, if you understand. It is the type of sermon I intend to preach when I am ordained."

He enthused on the subject for several moments, and Phoebe tried to think of a sermon she had read that might compare.

"Have you ever read anything by George Whitefield? My father heard him preach once when he was in America. He said Mr. Whitefield was the most captivating preacher he ever heard. He said that even Benjamin Franklin, who isn't a religious man, was impressed by Mr. Whitefield."

"Aye, that is true. Mr. Whitefield is likely one of the greatest preachers of modern times. I've never heard him myself, but I've read some of his sermons, and talked to people who have heard him. Now Whitefield is very different from Jonathan Edwards, you understand. Mr. Edwards read his speeches, and didn't try to impress people with his oratory. Mr. Whitefield is more like an actor. I'm not sure what I think about preachers trying to be actors. I think the Word of God should speak for itself and shouldn't be dressed up in a fancy style."

For several minutes he treated Phoebe to a lecture on the other differences between Edwards and Whitefield. If nothing else, he had certainly given the matter a good deal of thought. But then the conversation turned to politics and the war effort, and any sympathy Phoebe might have found for Miles Quincy vanished when he gave as his decided opinion that Congress had been precipitate in its break with England, and they would all live to regret the signing of the Declaration of Independence. Neither Edmund nor Alice disputed this opinion, and feeling herself outnumbered, she lapsed into silence, and made no more effort to be agreeable than politeness demanded. When they at long last arrived at home, she thanked the two men for the excursion and then vanished indoors, hoping she would not be obliged to repeat it.

On Thursday evening Phoebe returned home after delivering a bottle of medicine to one of her father's customers. As she stepped through the front door she heard voices in the parlor and her mother speaking in eager, happy tones. It was, she reflected, many weeks since she had heard her mother sound so excited.

She opened the parlor door and found the whole family gathered there, her father with his Bible on his lap, but not reading, Sally with her sampler and Alice clicking her knitting needles. She picked up the book she had left lying on a table and started for a chair, and then stopped in her tracks, for seated on the settee was Nicholas.

For a very brief moment their eyes met, then they both looked away. Phoebe felt the warmth rise in her face and glanced at her mother uncertainly.

"Phoebe, we have wonderful news!" her mother exclaimed. "Nicholas has brought us news of George!"

Phoebe turned to Nicholas, her embarrassment swallowed up in joy. "You have seen George?"

"I saw him briefly just a few days ago," Nicholas told her. "We didn't have the opportunity to speak, but he was certainly alive and healthy, and I thought your family might be cheered to hear of it."

"Oh, I am so relieved!" Sarah clasped her hands together with an expression close to rapture. "I am so thankful! Such a burden off of my mind! And I am more obliged to you than I can express, Nicholas dear, for making an effort to let us know."

"I am very happy to oblige you, ma'am," Nicholas responded, and Phoebe scarcely dared look to see the expression on his face. "I'm pleased it was in my power to deliver such welcome news."

Her mother turned to her and lowered her voice. "Phoebe dear, if you are not busy just now, could you run upstairs and put clean linen on George's bed?"

"Is George coming home soon?" Phoebe glanced from her mother to Nicholas for confirmation.

"Nay, not George, but Nicholas will be sleeping here while he is in town. There's no reason for him to stay in a filthy inn when we have an extra bed here."

Phoebe, watching Nicholas, saw his face redden as he met her gaze and looked away quickly.

"Certainly, Mother," she murmured, and turned toward the door, a confusion of emotions swirling through her middle. *Really, Lord,* she declared in silence as she fetched clean linen from the chest and began tightening the ropes on George's bed, *you've put me in an impossible situation. I wanted to know if Nicholas was still alive, but I certainly didn't want him living under the same roof with me. How terribly awkward.* And she knew her mother certainly would not welcome him so warmly if she guessed he had designs on one, or both, of her daughters. Had she been wrong to not tell her mother about that day in the woods? And what were his intentions now? How he must be enjoying the irony of this situation! How he would enjoy watching her squirm!

Her sleep that night was filled with very peculiar dreams, and she woke feeling tired and cross. While her mother busied herself with the younger children, Phoebe went to the kitchen to start breakfast, mixing the milk and porridge and setting it over the fire to boil.

The kitchen door opened and male footsteps entered. "Good morning, Phoebe," Nicholas said.

She hated the way the sound of his voice made her heart skip a beat. "Good morning, Nicholas." She kept her voice very cool. *If he smirks, even one tiny smirk, I shall be so tempted to slap his face.*

She turned around then, and met his gaze. He did not smirk. He seemed embarrassed, unsure of himself, odd, for Nicholas.

"Do you need any help?" He glanced around the kitchen.

Surprised, she started to refuse, then changed her mind. "You can lay the board if you'd like."

He found the bowls and began dropping them around on the table. Phoebe stirred the porridge.

"You know," he began awkwardly after a moment of silence, "your mother invited me to stay here. I had no idea she would do that."

"Nor did I," she replied. Better make that clear right from the beginning, in case he wondered.

He hesitated. "I suppose that means—I mean, you never told her about—that day?"

"Nay," Phoebe returned crisply, "but I certainly would, if it ever happened again."

At that he laughed, his old familiar laugh, with the crinkles around his eyes. "Never fear. I don't need to be told twice. I don't go where I'm not welcome."

Phoebe felt a sudden lifting of a weight, although she could not have explained exactly why. Perhaps it was relief that she and Nicholas understood each other. She remembered her letter to Lavinia, which now seemed totally unnecessary, but with any luck Nicholas would never find out about that. For an instant she felt a stab of apprehension that her mother might mention it to him. "Tell me about the war, Nicholas," she said, ready to move to an impersonal subject. "Is it as bad as people say?"

His face darkened. "It is bad. Morale has never been lower, and men are deserting left and right. We've been totally pushed out of the city, except for Fort Washington, which the British are besieging. I don't know if they can capture the fort, but I also don't know what good it does for us to keep it. We need those men with the army."

They were interrupted then by other family members coming to the kitchen for breakfast, and Phoebe returned her attention to the meal. After breakfast Nicholas told them he needed to rejoin the army that day, but he would be in the city again in several weeks.

He turned to Sarah. "I have a week of leave coming to me, and I wonder if I might trespass on your hospitality once again."

"You are welcome here anytime, Nicholas," she assured him, and actually offered him a motherly embrace. Phoebe had never seen Nicholas so flustered.

I had better get used to seeing him here, she reflected as she carried the bowls to the wash basin. *He doesn't seem to have any intention of avoiding me, and I have no way of avoiding him. I must learn to regard him as an indifferent acquaintance.*

But she soon discovered, to her sorrow, that she would need to get used to the presence of more than one young man. Several days later, as the mother and sisters were sewing together in the evening, Sarah told them both that Miles Quincy had asked for permission to court Phoebe.

Phoebe looked up, startled, from the mending in her lap. Her mother was beaming, and Alice smiled at the news, as if well satisfied.

"I expected he would," she nodded. "Edmund says he is eager to marry as soon as he is ordained, and we both thought he would be the perfect husband for Phoebe."

Phoebe was so appalled she was speechless.

"Phoebe a minister's wife!" Laughing, their mother snipped her length of thread. "Who would have imagined it? Well, stranger things have happened, and it shows that Phoebe's prospects might not be so dismal after all. But Phoebe, dear, now that you've made this conquest, I do hope you will settle down and behave like a young lady, and try to impress Mr. Quincy with your ability to think on serious subjects."

Phoebe had no intention of trying to impress Mr. Quincy with any of her abilities. She felt as if the breath had been knocked out of her, and sat in stunned silence until Alice rose and went to the kitchen to check on the bread that was rising.

Finally she spoke, in a very low voice. "Has Papa already told Mr. Quincy he may court me?"

Sarah looked up from Sally's petticoat, puzzled. "He told Mr. Quincy he wanted to consult with me first. But Alice vouches for this young man's good character, and I see no reason to refuse him."

"I don't want him to call on me." Phoebe stared down at the tiny stitches in her lap. "I don't want him to court me, or marry me, or anything. I don't like him."

"Don't like him!" Sarah dropped her sewing in her lap and stared at her daughter. "Phoebe, what nonsense are you talking? You've only met the man twice. You don't even know him. What is there not to like?"

Phoebe wet her lips and swallowed. "Perhaps I shouldn't have said I don't like him. I'm sure he is a very worthy young man. But—he's not interesting. I don't enjoy talking to him. I don't find him—attractive."

"Attractive!" Sarah picked up the needle and jabbed it through the petticoat with swift thrusts. "Attractive! That shows, Phoebe, just how childish you are being about this. Do you think a good marriage is built on good looks or a lively personality? Do you think that because a man is good-looking he will make you a good husband? No, Phoebe, a good marriage is built on good character. That is what you should be seeking in a man, and the fact that you don't seem to understand that makes me realize how much you have to learn about this subject."

"I know character is important," Phoebe protested, feeling tears sting her eyes at her mother's rebuke. "But shouldn't I also really like the person I have to marry?"

Her mother shot her a glance of exasperation. "Perhaps your expectations are too high. Alice doesn't find anything objectionable in Mr. Quincy."

"He isn't courting Alice!" Phoebe burst out. "Alice considers him acceptable for *me,* but she would never care for him that way *herself.* And what about the time Tom Kirby wanted to court Alice, and she objected? You didn't force her to see Tom!"

"You and Alice are as different as night and day, Phoebe. Alice has good judgment, and you do not. Tom Kirby is a fine boy, and I had no particular objection to him, but I also considered it likely that Alice would be able to make a better match if she tried, and so I allowed her to use her own judgment."

"And I cannot!" Phoebe cried. "You think if I don't accept Miles Quincy I will never find anyone else!"

"I didn't say that, Phoebe." For a moment her mother actually sounded flustered. "But the truth is you haven't had men knocking down our door, and I won't let you throw away the one likely prospect you have. And if you are thinking of Nicholas Teasdale, I beg you to put him out of your mind. He is a very pleasing young man, but Alice spoke the truth when she said that his family will look higher than us for marriage now that his father has made a fortune. If he were planning to court one of you, he would have chosen Alice, but he has never asked your father for either of you."

Phoebe felt a burning in her chest and a burning behind her eyes. "I know Nicholas isn't for me," she began, "This has nothing to do—" and then a thickness in her throat prevented her from speaking. She threw down her mending and ran out of the parlor and up to her room, where she threw herself down on her bed.

She wasn't crying over Miles Quincy or Nicholas Teasdale either, she told herself as she wiped her tears on her quilt. She would force herself to spend time with Miles if that would please her mother, although she couldn't imagine ever falling in love with him. As for Nicholas, she knew he had no interest in her beyond a romp in the grass. It was her mother's contempt for her that was so painful, her mother's contemptuous way of comparing her with Alice, the implication that she would never find another man and needed to grab at the first one who offered for her. She had always known that Alice came first in the family, that Alice was the most important, the most admired, and had tacitly accepted her second-place position, but she had never heard her mother express it in such hurtful terms.

She recalled Nicholas's question: "Do God and your mother always agree?"

Phoebe sat up and scrubbed her face with her handkerchief. *This once, just this once, Mother is wrong.*

ℰ ℭ

Phoebe had nearly forgotten about her letter to Lavinia Teasdale when an answer arrived. She felt a bit foolish whenever she remembered it. Now that she knew Nicholas was alive and well, her chief concern was that he might hear she had written to his sister and find it amusing. But at the same time, with the letter in her hand, she felt a good deal of pleasure and curiosity to know what Lavinia had written. She carried it up to her bedroom where she could read in private, and broke the seal.

My dear Phoebe,

> I was so surprised and pleased to hear from you again after the passage of so many years, and happy to hear your family are well and in good health. I often remember your family when we come into the city to visit my grandparents, and have wished for the opportunity to pay you a visit. I do especially hope that your brother George has come safely through the most recent battles and that you receive word of him soon. This war is a dreadful thing.

> A sad event has occurred in our family since we last corresponded. My brother Philip was wounded at Lexington. My parents arranged to bring him home, thinking his wound was trifling, but it afterward became infected, and he died last May. My parents are both quite grief-stricken over this event, and doubly grieved by my second brother's behavior.

65

When you met Nicholas in town, he, no doubt, did not explain his situation with regards to our family. The fact is that we have not seen or heard from Nicholas in over a year, since shortly after Philip's death. He and my father had a terrible row. I don't know all the details, but it centered on the fact that my father is a Loyalist and Nicholas planned to join the Rebel cause. (Philip fought with a Loyalist militia.) They exchanged hard words, and Nicholas left, and my father refuses to speak of him to anyone.

My mother, I know, is especially pained over this rift in the family, and misses Nicholas all the more acutely from having lost Philip as well. I pity her very much. I know she prays for him faithfully, and when I showed her your letter she was greatly comforted to hear that Nicholas is still alive and has contact with some of our former acquaintances. If you have any more news of Nicholas, I know my mother would be relieved to hear of it.

How fortunate you are, Phoebe, if your family has not been divided by this dreadful war as mine has been!

My mother is calling me now, so I must close this letter. I hope to send a longer one next time, and until then remain

Your affectionate friend

Lavinia Teasdale

&ↄ *Chapter Six* ℭℬ

Miles Quincy came to call on Phoebe that Sunday afternoon. Phoebe made coffee and served cakes, and then the two of them sat side by side on the settee in the parlor next to the blazing fire and tried to converse. Miles blushed and fumbled and stammered and mumbled in his rumbly deep voice, and Phoebe pasted a smile on her face and tried not to appear too fidgety. She wished she had brought some needlework to keep her hands busy and her eyes away from her suitor, and made a mental note to remember the next time, for she feared there would indeed be a next time. She suspected this was Mr. Quincy's first essay into courtship, and it seemed too cruel to reject him outright on his first attempt, for he might never wrack up the courage to try again. Besides which, her mother would never forgive her, and so she resigned herself to endure many uncomfortable Sunday afternoons. Surely in a few weeks, or months at the longest, Mr. Quincy himself would conclude that Phoebe was far from his picture of the ideal minister's wife.

It was so terribly unlucky, she reflected many times in vexation, that Miles Quincy's courtship was not of a nature to help her put Nicholas Teasdale out of her mind. Unfortunately, Nicholas appeared so attractive in comparison that it required all her good sense and self-control to keep from repining. Surely somewhere in the world there was some man who combined Nicholas's liveliness and charm with Miles's sterling character, although, if her mother's judgment was reliable, such a man would not give Phoebe a second look anyway.

During the third week in November, news of the surrender of Fort Washington to the British flew from mouth to mouth. Phoebe knew neither George nor Nicholas was involved in the defense of the fort; nevertheless, it was a humiliating loss for the Rebel forces. Few men had actually been killed, but nearly three thousand were captured by the British. Rhoda Kirby confided to her that her brother Tom was among the captured.

"How dreadful!" Phoebe embraced her friend, her sympathy heightened as she remembered her mother's fear for George and her own anxiety during the uncertainty at Brooklyn Heights. "Your poor mother! Poor Betsy! Have you told her about this?"

Rhoda dismissed Betsy with a wave of the hand. "She has a new suitor now, a Quaker fellow her parents approve. Oh, poor Tom! Papa says we had no business trying to defend that fort. How could Washington have made such a clumsy mistake? Three thousand men gone! And more deserting every day! I heard Papa and his friends say last night that Congress made a dreadful decision when they appointed General Washington as commander-in-chief. Mr. Norton said they should have chosen Charles Lee instead. *He* at least has some experience in European wars."

Phoebe felt sincere sympathy over Tom's capture, but knew not what to say about Washington. She knew Nicholas greatly admired Washington, but it did seem that during the last three months the army had nearly disintegrated under his leadership. One dreadful loss after another, and now this! And the next Sunday when Miles Quincy came courting, he concurred with Mr. Kirby's opinion, adding that one more battle would finish off the Rebel cause for good, that only a miracle could save it now. This view did nothing to endear him to Phoebe, but at the same time she had to concede there was some validity to it.

She had thought of Nicholas more or less continually ever since the advent of Lavinia's letter. His sister's explanation made some things clear to Phoebe, and yet opened up a whole new set of questions. She had to admire Nicholas for standing by his convictions in spite of his father's opposition, but was this alone the root of his rebellious attitude, his resentment against his father that had surfaced that one afternoon, even the cynicism toward God and religion that she had often sensed?

It was a bit peculiar that he had never mentioned his estrangement from his family—even his own brother's death! More importantly, *why* had he and his father fallen out so completely? Was it simply because of their differing political views?

She longed to ask him these questions, but could not do so very easily without mentioning Lavinia's letter. Besides, she knew it was really none of her business, and if Nicholas had never brought up the subject he must not care to discuss it. It was her duty to keep her distance from him, not to become embroiled in his family quarrel which she could do nothing to resolve anyway. But all these sensible reflections did not squelch her curiosity or her solicitude.

During the last week of November Nicholas arrived at the Fuller household to spend his leave. Phoebe greeted him along with the rest of the family and then left the room as soon as she was able to think of a reasonable excuse. She would *not*, she resolved firmly, linger near him all week waiting for a word or a smile, or make any excuse at all to speak with him. She wondered how long he intended to stay with them.

"I truly don't understand Nicholas coming here to spend his leave," Alice remarked that night as she and Phoebe undressed for bed. "Why wouldn't he spend it with his own family? They don't live any farther from the army than we do."

Phoebe shrugged and made a non-committal reply. That much at least made sense to her now after Lavinia's letter, but she had never shared any of it with her family. She wasn't sure whether or not she should.

The next evening Edmund and Miles came together to visit with Alice and Phoebe. At least, Phoebe thought ruefully as she greeted her suitor, having the four of them together would make the situation a bit more enjoyable. They all repaired to the parlor and, at Edmund's suggestion, gathered around the harpsichord to listen to Alice play. Phoebe was pleased with the arrangement, for it would be unnecessary to carry on a conversation while someone was entertaining them with music. She managed one smile in Miles's direction and then settled back to listen with a kerchief that she was embroidering.

When Alice had finished two pieces, Nicholas entered the parlor, and she looked up from her music.

"Please don't let me interrupt you." Nicholas glanced around the room with a smile that included them all. "I was hoping to use your father's desk to make a copy of a letter from my commander. But if this is an inconvenient time, please tell me so. I can wait till tomorrow."

"If my playing doesn't distract you," Alice told him, gesturing toward the desk in the corner. "Please, feel free."

Nicholas smiled at them all again, and Phoebe fancied for just a second that his glance lingered on Miles, sizing him up. But perhaps that was just her imagination.

He sat down and opened the desk, and Alice began to play again. This time she chose some of the hymns from the Methodist service, and they sang along with the lively modern tunes: "Love Divine, all Loves Excelling," "Rock of Ages," and "O For a Thousand Tongues to Sing my Great Redeemer's Praise." Nicholas finished the letter and left the room, and then Alice paused in her playing and suggested that Phoebe fetch them some refreshments.

Phoebe willingly rose and went to the kitchen, and as she passed the desk she noticed Nicholas had left the letter lying unsealed. She brewed coffee, dawdling as long as possible in the task, then added bread and strawberry preserves to the tray and carefully carried the load back to the parlor. But as she passed the desk she noticed the letter was gone.

She began to serve the coffee around the room, then spread a slice of bread with preserves and settled back in her chair to sip and nibble and listen to the men talk about acquaintances of theirs of whom she had no knowledge and less interest. In a moment Nicholas reappeared. She saw him search the desk for the letter, but couldn't find it. He frowned, glancing around the room at the two men, and then caught Phoebe's eye. She frowned back at him and spread her hands to show she didn't know where the letter had vanished to. Nicholas seated himself again and picked up the quill.

It was certainly odd. Had Edmund taken Nicholas's letter? Or Miles? But that was absurd. Why would either of them do such a thing? The letter had been written by Lord Stirling, Nicholas had said. It probably contained information about the war. Neither Edmund nor Miles was involved in the war in any way. Of course, Phoebe did not know Miles well at all. But he was seated on the far side of Edmund; he could not easily have confiscated the letter without his friend's notice.

She glanced back at Nicholas and saw him studying the room carefully, a thoughtful, enigmatic expression on his face. When he met her gaze he lifted his eyebrows and smiled at her, the sort of smile that had always struck Phoebe as either mocking or amused.

She glanced away, mentally shrugging. It was none of her business, anyway.

ℬ ℭ

Nicholas slid into the dim alley beside the tavern, lifted the lid of the crate, and groped in its darkened interior. For a moment he felt nothing, then realized the paper was standing up on its side, not lying flat. He snatched it up and stuffed it into his pocket, then strolled out of the alley and down the street. After rounding the block once, he opened the tavern door and entered.

It took a moment for his eyes to adjust to the light within. He heard a servant call, "Good evening, Mr. Teasdale," and turned in the direction of the voice.

"Evening, Jenny. You're rather busy here tonight, aren't you?'

"Aye, we've been jumping all evening. Are you looking for some supper, sir?"

"I've already eaten," Nicholas told her. "I just want a drink."

The pretty, buxom girl laughed. "Just looking for some company, hey?"

Nicholas smiled. "You could say that." He glanced around the room until his gaze picked out three figures at a table against the wall. "As a matter of fact, I think I've found my company."

He strolled over to the table. Edmund Ingram looked up and surprise registered on his face.

"Ingram! And Mr. Quincy, if I remember rightly." Nicholas bowed to the three men in turn. "What a coincidence! I never imagined to meet you fellows here!"

Observing Edmund narrowly, he saw the man's expression of surprise become thoughtful, calculating, before he smiled. Edmund rose to his feet, bowed, and gestured to the chair across from him.

"It certainly is a pleasant surprise. Come join us, if you will."

"Thank you. I hope I don't intrude." Nicholas dropped into the proffered chair and studied the stocky, muscular man seated next to Edmund, wearing the waistcoat and fine shirt of a gentleman. In spite of his elegant clothes, he was rather red-faced and sweating, either because of the heat of the tavern or quantity of liquor he had already imbibed. "I'm afraid I'm not acquainted with your friend."

"Excuse my manners. This is Mr. Harry Hastings, a merchant here in town. Harry, this is Nicholas Teasdale, an officer in the fine army of George Washington."

Nicholas saw Harry barely cover a smirk as the two men nodded to each other. "Pleased to make your acquaintance."

"Join us for a drink." Edmund poured a tankard full of the heady dark liquid in the pitcher and pushed it toward Nicholas. "My compliments."

So that's the idea. Get me liquored up and hope I babble like an idiot. Although from the nearly empty pitcher Nicholas guessed one of others might start babbling first. He turned to the servant who was passing by the table. "Jenny, could you bring me some coffee, please? Or better yet, do you have any chocolate?"

"So tell me, Teasdale." Edmund took a long swig from the glass in front of him. "How do you come to be staying with the Fullers? Old friend of the family, Alice tells me."

"That's true." Nicholas nodded around the circle of men. "We were neighbors as children, and I often visit when I'm in town." His gaze rested briefly on Miles Quincy. So that was the fellow who was courting Phoebe. Of course one shouldn't judge by appearances, the man might be a brilliant conversationalist, but he couldn't help but wonder what the attraction was.

"Don't have your eye on either of the daughters, I assume," Edmund persisted. "Pure friendship, hey?"

Nicholas accepted the mug of chocolate from Jenny with a smile and took a sip.

"Just a friend of the family. Nothing more."

"Lucky for you, hey, Miles?" Edmund lifted his glass to his friend. "You wouldn't want this brave officer of General Washington stealing your little sweetheart away, now would you?"

Harry Hastings laughed a raucous laugh while Miles smiled an uncomfortable smile and Nicholas almost felt sorry for him. He took another sip of chocolate. Edmund certainly didn't seem worried about anyone stealing his own sweetheart away, he noted.

"Oh, Miles doesn't have a thing to worry about," Harry laughed. "He's become quite the ladies' man now that he's courting. Tell us all about it, Miles. Does little Phoebe give you calf's eyes? Has she ever kissed you? What else has she given you? Come on, we're all men. You can tell us all the details."

Edmund hooted with laughter while Nicholas bit hard on his lip, keeping his expression perfectly blank to hide his contempt. For just a moment that day back in August flashed before his eyes, filling him with shame and then outrage. If Miles ever, ever—no, he wouldn't believe it. He should give Phoebe credit for better sense than that.

Miles seemed confused by the banter of his friends. He glanced from one to the other and then at Nicholas, his expression uncertain.

"I've never tried to kiss her. Do you think I should do that? I don't want to offend her."

"Offend her!" Edmund's voice held a note of mock surprise. "Why Miles, she's probably hoping you'll try something! She's probably disappointed that you haven't!"

Miles's face brightened. "Do you really think so?"

Harry was laughing too hard to speak. He took another swig of rum and almost choked before he swallowed.

"I think Miles just needs a few lessons. Hey, let me show you how 'tis done."

He gestured to the servant and Jenny approached the table. "Can I fetch something for you, sir?"

Harry stood up, snatched Jenny in his arms, and laid a long kiss on her pretty mouth. Jenny jerked back out of his arms and flounced away. Harry pinched her backside as she escaped.

"There's a lesson for you, Miles my boy!" Harry dropped back into his chair and lifted his glass again. "Try that with your little Phoebe next time you go courting!"

Nicholas tried to laugh, but it was a forced, awkward laugh. He hoped the other men didn't notice and think he was odd. After all, it was no different than the sort of rowdiness he had often indulged in himself. Edmund shot him a keen glance.

"Watch yourself, there, Harry. Teasdale is an old friend of the

Fuller family. Practically a brother, one might say. He might find it his duty to defend the family honor."

"I'm terrified." Harry took another drink. "He'll no doubt defend their honor the same way his fellow rebels defended Fort Washington."

Edmund shot Harry a warning glance. Nicholas took another long sip of his chocolate and carefully wiped his mouth with his napkin. It was strange, he mused. When one wasn't drinking oneself, there was really nothing so obnoxious as a drunk.

"So tell us all about the war effort, Teasdale." Edmund's tone was casual. "You fellows have had a rough few months, haven't you?"

Nicholas thought of the condition of the army as he had just left it, nearly disintegrating before his eyes. Not enough food, not enough blankets, not enough ammunition. Widespread hopelessness had replaced the earlier excitement.

He shrugged, keeping his expression matter-of-fact. "The last few months have been difficult. The capture of the fort didn't help. The army is smaller than we'd like, probably no more than ten thousand men. But we have new recruits coming in every day."

"Ten thousand men!" Edmund stared at him in disbelief. "Three thousand were lost at Fort Washington, and you still have ten thousand men?"

"Perhaps not quite ten thousand." He knew full well that five thousand was a more realistic estimate. "The number might be closer to nine thousand. But the men love Washington, and they'd do anything for him. And as I said, more men are pouring in every day. We need to regroup, and then we'll start pushing the redcoats back up to New York." The reality was that no one was pouring in—rather, men were deserting in droves. He knew, as well as anyone, the widespread doubts about Washington's ability and the talk of replacing him with another general.

Harry glanced at Edmund, but Edmund was staring down into his rum, looking pensive.

"Perhaps I should even join the fight," he mused. "I've thought of it, you know, from time to time, even though I have no real fondness for war. I despise the way the Hessians have treated the people of New Jersey. I'd like to be there when the redcoats get pushed back up to New York."

Nicholas lowered his eyes to his mug to conceal the contempt that he felt. "Aye, that you should. With your training you could become a clerk or a courier."

Harry let out a loud guffaw. "How rich! Ingram as a clerk to George Washington! How I'd love to see that! Wouldn't *all* your friends love that!"

Edmund shot his friend an angry glance of warning which Nicholas pretended not to notice. Harry was becoming too intoxicated to guard his tongue.

"Give your friend more credit," Nicholas returned, appearing to misunderstand him. "Sometimes the studious, learned types can be a great benefit to the army. Mr. Ingram here is probably a man of many hidden talents. He could be extremely useful in this war if he chose to be."

Edmund threw Nicholas a sharp glance. Nicholas met his gaze and smiled a benign smile.

"The war has found assistance in some of the most unlikely places," Nicholas continued. "We have men in New York from old Tory families who use their connections to glean information about Howe's plans and pass them along to us. Although, from what I hear, General Howe is more interested in Mrs. Loring than he is in actually fighting this war."

Edmund leaned forward, his eyes alert, then lowered his gaze as if to conceal his curiosity. He waved to Jenny to refill the pitcher of rum. "How very interesting. I'm sure you must hear many such stories in your position. Serving under Lord Stirling as you do. I believe that's what you said—Lord Stirling?"

Nicholas nodded. "That's correct."

"And these men in New York," Edmund lowered his voice to an almost confidential tone, "I'm sure they can't be from really influential families. I mean, you would never be able to recruit such men as spies, you know."

Nicholas hesitated, then glanced right and left as if afraid of being overheard. "I can't tell you much, of course. But I have heard a few names. Grant, Dunmore, Lewis—do those names mean anything to you?"

He saw Edmund's eyes widen, but he said nothing. Harry Hastings let out a loud whistle before he took another long drink.

"There you go, Ingram. I'm sure old Maxwell will be interested in hearing about *that*."

Edmund shot his friend a furious look which Nicholas carefully ignored. He glanced at Miles, who seemed befuddled by the whole conversation, and smiled a benevolent smile.

❧ *Chapter Seven* ❧

After supper the next day Phoebe carried the milk pail to the barn to milk the cow. It was a task she disliked, for the cow was temperamental and sometimes kicked, but tonight Buttercup was in an affable mood and stood calmly lowing as Phoebe milked. She was nearly finished when the barn door opened and Nicholas entered.

He went to his horse and began to saddle him. Phoebe glanced over her shoulder at him, and their eyes met.

"Is Buttercup behaving today?" he asked.

She laughed and nodded, surprised that he remembered the cow's name. "Are you going for a ride?"

"Aye, I thought Syllabub could use the exercise, and so could I."

She turned back to her task. "Did you ever find your letter?"

"Letter?" For a moment he seemed to have forgotten. "Nay. I recopied it."

"Oh." He didn't seem concerned, so she dismissed the incident. "How odd."

"Aye, it is indeed."

There was a pause. Phoebe stood up and started to pick up the milk pail, when Nicholas said, "So who is this Quincy fellow anyway?"

She stopped and glanced back at him. "He—he's a friend of Edmund's."

"Is he really courting you?"

"Who says so?"

"Jonathan."

"Oh." Phoebe shrugged. Nothing was secret with her younger brothers. "He did ask my papa for permission."

She picked up the pail and started for the door, when he spoke again. "Do you like him?"

Phoebe stopped and swung back to look at him. Nicholas was still tightening the saddle, his face averted. What could she say? "I'm trying to keep an open mind," she said carefully.

She had nearly reached the door when she heard Nicholas laugh shortly. "Please tell me he has money."

"Money?" Phoebe set down the milk pail. "What does that mean?"

"Well, he certainly isn't handsome, and he's as dull as ditchwater, but I reckon there must be some attraction."

"He's a minister," Phoebe replied in a tight voice. "That's attraction enough for my mother."

"A minister. I see now. Everyone knows ministers make the best husbands, after all."

There was that sarcastic edge to his voice she had noticed before. "My mother says that as long as he has good character, other types of attraction are not so important."

"What rubbish!" Nicholas burst out. "You aren't really going to marry him, are you, Phoebe?"

Phoebe had no intention of marrying Miles, but it was none of Nicholas's business. "I don't know. My mother thinks I am lucky to have him."

"Why don't you stand up to your mother for a change and tell her you are going to make your own decisions?"

"Just like you did with your father?"

The words were out of her mouth before she had a chance to stop them. She saw his face blanch with either anger or embarrassment, and it was a moment before he spoke.

"Who told you about that?"

She hesitated, but there was no point in prevaricating now. "Your sister."

"Lavinia wrote to you?"

"Aye."

"What did she tell you?"

"She—she told me you had quarreled with your father, and about your brother's death. Why didn't you tell us about that, Nicholas?"

He shrugged. "You didn't ask."

"But I did!" Phoebe burst out. Now that the subject was broached, she could not let him slither away like that. "I asked how your family fared, and you said they were all well. That was not very honest of you, Nicholas."

He shrugged again, but his face was hard. He swung up into the saddle. "Then add it to my other sins. You should know I have quite a list by now."

"Nicholas—" As he pushed past her she reached out to him, touching his ankle, but he kicked his horse and trotted out the door.

Phoebe listened to the rhythm of the horse's hooves until they faded away into the night. Well, she had certainly botched that conversation. But it was partly his fault for being so nosy about Miles. She picked up her milk pail and started back to the house, the milk sloshing over the top and wetting her petticoat.

Nicholas did not appear the rest of the evening, and the whole family went to bed at the normal hour, their mother wondering aloud where he might be. Phoebe lay awake after Alice and Sally were both breathing rhythmically in sleep and the house was silent.

She heard the trotting of a horse to the stable behind the house, then, a few moments later, the kitchen door opening. Suddenly in the stillness there was a clatter, and a muffled curse, as if someone had stumbled in the dark.

Phoebe sat up. Alice rolled over and was silent. In the rest of the house no one stirred.

On an impulse she climbed out of bed and pulled her petticoat on over her shift. She crept down the stairs, hoping not to waken her parents.

The kitchen was dark, but Phoebe found a candle stub and lit it in the smoldering embers of the fireplace. The pale flame showed Nicholas where he had dropped onto a kitchen bench and sat watching her, his eyes dark and circled.

"You are going to wake the whole family," she whispered.

"Sorry," he muttered. "I didn't realize it was so late."

She approached the kitchen table. Was he drunk? At least he

looked sober, but then she had little experience with drunken men. Was he, perhaps, upset over their earlier conversation? "Nicholas, I apologize for bringing up such an unpleasant subject earlier. I did not intend to mention it."

He shrugged again. "Don't fret about it, Phoebe. It was my fault for criticizing your mother and your lover."

She winced at hearing Miles described as her lover. "Your family is very concerned about you, Nicholas. Your mother particularly, Lavinia says."

She saw him flinch as the mention of his mother, and lowered his eyes. "I wish I could see her again. 'twas none of it her fault."

She opened her mouth to speak again, then closed it. She dropped down on the bench across from him. For a moment they sat in silence.

"Phoebe, do you know what it is like to always be second best?" The words burst out of him all at once. "To never be adequate? To always be less important? That's the way I felt, all my life, growing up. Philip was always my father's favorite, the good son, the important one. Everything with Philip came first. I was always second. Less clever, less handsome, less able. I could never measure up. I could only please my father by trying to be Philip, and that was impossible."

Phoebe said nothing, but listened in silence.

"One incident from my childhood always stands out in my mind. I suppose it was a silly thing, but I can never forget it. When I was fourteen our mare birthed a foal, and when the foal was big enough to ride I broke him myself. I remember we had guests one evening, and I rode the horse around the yard, showing off, I suppose, and everyone admired me. Everyone but my father, who said not a word. That day at dinner the lady complimented my achievement, but my father just changed the subject and started talking about Philip, who had started college, and what a scholar he was. And I thought, nothing I do will ever measure up, in his eyes, to what Philip can do."

"I can understand," Phoebe said quietly. "I'm sure that was hurtful."

He bit his lip for a moment before continuing. "By the time I reached my late teens I began to rebel, I suppose. If I couldn't be Philip, I would be as different from him as I possibly could. I began to indulge in certain behaviors that a good little Methodist girl like you would never approve." He managed a crooked grin at her. "And as the political situation worsened, since my father and brother were Loyalists, I took the other side. I really did believe in the cause, you understand, but I also took pleasure in opposing them. I suppose it was part of my rebellion too.

"When Philip finished college, my father asked him to stay in Boston and handle the business there as my father's partner. As the political problems grew, Philip joined a Loyalist militia that was supposed to help maintain order. How proud my father was! His son, defending the King, against all those ornery Rebels! But in April last year his militia rode out to help Lord Hugh Percy seize the supplies at Concord, and Philip was shot in the arm in the confrontation at Lexington. My parents managed to bring him home, hoping to nurse him back to health. They brought a doctor to him, who said the arm would need to be amputated, but Philip refused. He would rather die than live as half a man with only one arm. Three days later they fetched the doctor again, but it was too late. The gangrene had already spread too far to amputate. And Philip got his wish."

"How dreadful," Phoebe whispered. "I am so, so sorry."

"It *was* dreadful, in more ways than one." Nicholas clenched his teeth. "After Philip died, my father wanted me to move to Boston and take Philip's place in the business, and join the Loyalist militia. That way at least he would have one son fighting for his king, and he could be proud again. I told him that King George was not my king, and I had already decided to join the Continental Army. We had a terrible quarrel then; I don't even recall all the things that were said. But at one point I said," Nicholas paused, swallowing hard, staring down at his folded hands with their white knuckles, "I said, 'You wish Philip were still alive and I were lying down in the family plot,' and he said, 'Aye, I do; he was a son to be proud of and you are a disgrace.'"

"Oh, Nicholas." Phoebe reached her hand to him, horrified and saddened. "You know he didn't mean it. He was speaking out of his grief and anger."

"Aye, he was angry and grief-stricken, but he meant it. 'Twas the truest thing he ever said to me. And at that point I told him I was leaving and never coming back. So I left, and I haven't returned since."

Their eyes met across the table, his anguished and defiant, hers sorrowful. "I think you broke your mother's heart," she said softly.

"I'm certain of it," he sighed. "But what could I do?"

"I don't know." She shook her head. "Don't you miss your family at all?"

He shrugged. "Aye, but I cannot go back. Nothing I do will ever please him."

Phoebe hesitated, reluctant to give advice in such a situation, and yet struggling to frame her thoughts into words. "Perhaps you are right, Nicholas. Perhaps you will never please your father. But you can look above him and do what is right, whether he ever approves or not."

"Look above him? What do you mean? How can I do that?"

"It is not my place to tell you God's plan for you," Phoebe said slowly, groping for the right words, "But the most important thing is for you to be at peace with Him."

For just a second she expected another mocking comment, but Nicholas folded his hands, resting his chin on them, and stared off above her head in deep thought.

"I know that you are a real Christian, Phoebe," he said finally. "But for me, God was just another person who was always disappointed in me.

"Your father isn't God, Nicholas," she told him. "God accepts you, he loves you, even if your father doesn't."

He was silent for a long moment, staring at her intently. "I find that difficult to believe," he said finally.

Phoebe fell silent. If she were someone else, more intelligent, articulate, or devout, perhaps she could reason with Nicholas further, but she found herself at a loss.

"You and I have different tempers," he went on. "Call it pride, arrogance, whatever, but I cannot humble myself the way you do. When Alice or someone else in your family puts you down, you accept it, and I want to fight back."

Phoebe remembered his criticism of her in the barn. "You think I am too meek?"

He shrugged. "My way has never been the model for Christian behavior; who am I to criticize? But I sometimes feel your humility is really a lack of confidence in yourself, in your judgment and abilities."

"Perhaps you are right," she said slowly, and then, on an impulse, recounted her quarrel with her mother over Miles Quincy, omitting her mother's reference to Nicholas himself. "I must confess, it hurt me very much that her opinion of Alice is so much higher than her opinion of me."

Nicholas nodded. "Aye, that is exactly what I mean. As if you don't have the good judgment to choose a worthy man on your own."

Pheobe stared down at the board cloth and traced a circular pattern with her finger. "Perhaps I don't."

He leaned across the table then, and to her amazement covered her hand with his own. His touch was warm and strong, his palm and fingertips callused. "Aye, you do, Phoebe." He smiled at her gently. "As I well know, to my own disappointment. As Quincy will surely find out. You are too pretty to settle for someone you dislike, and too wise to let yourself be hoodwinked by some clever rogue who might try to take advantage of you."

For a long moment they sat looking at each other, their gazes locked, and then Phoebe lowered hers to the table top. Nicholas withdrew his hand and pushed back the bench with a scraping sound.

"And on that note," he added, rising to his feet, "I think we both need to find our beds before we awaken your whole family."

༅ ༀ

Winter arrived soon after Nicholas departed to rejoin the army, and along with the cold weather came the Continental Army to the banks of the Delaware, in an ignominious flight from the enemy across New Jersey. During the second week of December word reached Philadelphia that Washington's army had collected sufficient boats and crossed the river, camping north of the city. The citizens trembled and a sense of dread fell over the town, for the enemy would surely be close behind, and there was little doubt in anyone's mind that Philadelphia was their quest.

"Once the British get to Philadelphia, this rebellion will be over," Phoebe heard Edmund remark to Alice as they sat in the parlor together one evening. "And that won't be long now. Congress has run away, and they wouldn't do that if they didn't believe the King's men would be here soon. And they granted the powers of a military dictatorship to

Washington! Didn't I say Washington would end up as another Cromwell if the rebels win this war? It's beginning already!"

Phoebe remembered their previous conversation on the subject, back in September. Edmund had said then that Washington simply wanted political power and that he would eventually become a dictator like all other military conquerors. Could Edmund be right? She knew very little about Washington, or the members of Congress, for that matter—she knew none of them personally. Maybe they really did just want money and power. Would they bully and oppress and exploit middling families like the Fullers if they were able to overthrow the British in America? Or did they really believe in the ideals they were disseminating in revolutionary writings like the Declaration of Independence and *Common Sense*? How could an average girl like Phoebe ever be sure?

Alice shuddered, stabbing her needle through the ripped breeches she was mending. "I just pray the British get here first, and not the Hessians. Surely they'll treat us better. Don't you believe so?"

"Of course." Edmund smiled and pushed a stray piece of her golden hair back into place. "Don't be afraid. I don't think you need to worry about anything."

"But the Hessians are right across the river in Trenton! How do we know they won't wipe out Washington's army and treat us the same way they're treating all the people in New Jersey? Or maybe Washington's men will just run away like they've done a dozen times before. Oh, Edmund, I've been so scared I can't sleep at night! I just want this horrid conflict to be over so we can go back to life the way it was before!"

Phoebe knew Alice was far from alone in her fears. Rumors were flying rampant around the city and the population was close to panic.

One night in the middle of December Phoebe was wakened from a sound sleep by a banging on the front door. Glancing at the tiny window, she could see that it was still black outside. She and Alice sat up in bed and listened as their father's footsteps approached the door. They heard voices tense with alarm, and then their mother's voice rising above the others in fear. A moment later Sarah's footsteps came running up the stairs and into their room.

"Wake up, girls!" Their mother carried a burning pine knot, her face white and distorted in the flickering light. "We have to get dressed and start packing right away. General Washington is planning to burn the city to keep the British from seizing it."

Phoebe and Alice looked at each other in horror. "Burn the city?"

"Hurry." Sarah's voice was sharp. "Pack your clothes and make sure Sally packs hers as well. As soon as you are ready come downstairs and help me decide what we can take with us. Your father is hitching up the wagon. We don't have much time." She vanished through the door and Phoebe heard her waking the boys in the room across the hall.

Alice and Phoebe tumbled out of bed and pulled on petticoats and waistcoats. Still groggy from sleep, they gathered together their best clothes and packed them in a small trunk. When they finished, Alice hurried downstairs to help her mother while Phoebe went to her brothers' room to oversee their packing. Even her brothers were terrified by the war so close to their home. The five children piled their belongings by the front door and joined their mother around the kitchen table.

"How do we know when they plan to do this?" Alice's pretty face was paler than normal. "Surely they wouldn't set fire to the city without giving us all time to leave, would they?"

"Is our house going to burn?" Sally was close to tears.

"We don't know." Her mother's tone was more abrupt than normal. "That's why we need to be prepared. Your father has gone out to try to learn what he can."

For the next two hours they spoke in tense whispers and paced the floors and moved back and forth to the windows, awaiting their father's return. When he appeared he had little fresh intelligence to offer. He had not been able to either confirm or disprove the rumor, but he had seen no fires. Finally, as light appeared on the eastern horizon, the family returned to bed to snatch a few hours of sleep before the new day.

In the morning Sarah sent Phoebe to the Kirbys' house to learn what she could from her more enlightened friends. As Phoebe crossed the streets, she thought the city looked normal, but with fewer people outdoors, and a more subdued atmosphere than usual. A hush seemed to lie over the town, as if everyone were waiting for something and knew not what. But she saw no sign of fires, and could smell no smoke.

"We heard the rumors too, but my father is inclined to disbelieve them," Rhoda told Phoebe as she let her into the house. "He's gone out to contact his friends among the Associators to see what he can learn."

Phoebe waited for an hour, and was rewarded for her patience when Mr. Kirby returned home with an expression of great relief.

"General Putnam has denied there is any plan to burn the city," he informed his family. "It seemed like a mad notion to me in the first place. No one ever thought of burning New York, after all. It just shows how panicky everyone is, when these ridiculous rumors start from nothing at all."

The women exchanged glances of supreme relief. "Thank heaven," Mrs. Kirby sighed.

"Now all we have to worry about is the Hessians," Phoebe added.

Cries for Washington's replacement grew louder and stronger, and several days later Phoebe learned from Rhoda that some of the Philadelphia militia had been called to join the army, although her father's company had not been chosen.

"Papa says more and more men are deserting every day," Rhoda told her gravely, "and even worse, the ones who remain will have their terms expire at the end of the year. So on New Year's Day Washington might suddenly be left with no army at all."

"What a Christmas!" Phoebe sighed, comparing this cold, dismal month with its sense of dread and impending disaster to former happy, peaceful celebrations.

Her mother agreed. "I don't even want to celebrate Christmas this year," she told her husband that night at supper. "It doesn't seem right, with George in the army and this terrible war right on our doorstep."

"No Christmas?" Sally echoed, glancing from her mother to her father in dismay.

"I don't know," her father said slowly. "It is still the birthday of our Lord. Should we give thanks only when things are going well for us?"

Sarah was silent for a moment, then sighed. "At least I could invite my brother's family to share our dinner that day. 'Twould be a proper gesture, although I won't be in a holiday spirit."

"I have a surprise already planned for Christmas," her husband told them with a twinkle in his eye, but he refused to give them any hints. "We will have it by Christmas Eve."

ℰ *Chapter Eight* ℬ

Nicholas dug his coldest hand deep into his pocket and tried to manage the reins with his free one. He bent his head against the gust of wind which threatened to sweep away his cocked felt hat. Only December, and it already felt like February. What would February be like? Perhaps they would be lucky and spring would come early next year. But right now spring seemed very far away.

How far had he gone since the fork in the road? Had he made a wrong turn? Perhaps a mile back he had passed a farmhouse, with no sign of the inhabitants. Should he ride back and go to the door? With a little luck they might invite him inside to warm himself. But no, better to keep going. Surely he would pass another farm soon, or come to a village.

His ears perked up as the wind slackened for a minute and far off he could hear the trudge of footsteps and rattle of wheels on the road. Was it his imagination? He nudged Syllabub to a trot and was rewarded when he rounded the bend in the road and spotted a farmer coming toward him, driving a wagon filled with a load of wood. Nicholas reined in when he reached the side of his fellow traveler.

"Good day, friend." Nicholas lifted a hand in greeting. "Cold day today, isn't it?"

The man grunted in return.

"Perhaps you could tell me," Nicholas persisted, "am I on the road to the British camp? Is it far from here?"

"Blasted redcoats," the man grumbled. "All over this country like a flock of crows in harvest. Aye, you're on the right road. Just follow it another five miles or more, and you'll reach the camp."

"Thank you." Nicholas nodded farewell.

The man eyed him with suspicion or curiosity, Nicholas wasn't sure which. "You're a peddler, I take it?"

Nicholas laughed. "Aye, and I've found the redcoats have plenty of silver in their pockets. More than the rebels, for sure."

"Doesn't surprise me," the man mumbled. With a grunt to his mule he started his wagon.

Nicholas nudged Syllabub into motion again, relieved by this conversation. Although many residents of New Jersey had rushed to swear an oath of allegiance to the Crown, in reality they had no liking for the swarm of soldiers who had descended on their land. Both the British and Hessians had difficulty distinguishing between Whigs and Tories in their treatment of the locals, which did not endear them to either side.

Nearly an hour passed before he saw any sign of the British camp. He passed through a small village which resembled the countless small villages dotting the New Jersey countryside. A bit farther on he spotted a farmhouse surrounded by a bustle of activity, resembling a colony of red ants. The farmhouse had no doubt been commandeered by the British.

He pulled Syllabub to a halt and took a deep breath, his heart beginning to race under the rough kersey shirt he wore. Gone was the uniform which had been the envy of so many lesser men in the ranks. Instead he wore the clothes of a laborer: leather breeches, worsted stockings with gaiters, and a kerchief around his neck under his heavy coat. Surely he looked the part. Surely no one would guess. No one had so far. And he carried no papers to reveal his identity. His only real danger would be if he happened to meet with someone who recognized him. And that was not at all likely.

He told himself these things every time before he rode into a British camp, but he could not completely dispel the feeling that he was putting his head into a noose, that he only had a few seconds before the noose would tighten and he could no longer withdraw it.

God help me, he prayed. *I've never been much of a Christian, I know. Maybe I don't have the right to ask for help. But Lord, if you care about me at all, help me to get in and out of this camp safely.*

He knew he should move; he knew he should approach the camp before someone spotted him and wondered what he was doing, loitering there on the road outside. Quelling the nervous dance in his stomach, he rode forward to the wagon path that led from the road to the farmhouse. A pair of sentries stopped him and one spoke.

"What is your business here?" The man spoke with an odd accent unlike any Nicholas was familiar with in the colonies. *How strange,* he reflected. *Here in America we are even beginning to talk differently from the people in England.*

He dismounted, holding Syllabub by the reins. "I have tobacco for sale. The best tobacco, straight from Virginia. Excellent snuff and pipe tobacco. Do you want to see?"

Before they could object, he opened his saddlebags and pulled out a sample of his wares. One of the men leaned closer and sniffed; Nicholas could smell his rancid breath. The two sentries exchanged a glance.

"We need to search him," one of them said.

Nicholas laughed. "I'd be happy to strip down to my breeches for you fellows, but 'tis beastly cold out here. Is there somewhere warmer we could go? I'd be grateful to get out of this wind."

One of the sentries opened Nicholas's coat, stuck his hands in his pockets, and patted him for weapons and the crinkling of paper. Nicholas took his knife from his pocket and displayed it for them. "This is the only weapon I carry, friends," he smiled.

The sentries seemed to relax, disarmed by his geniality. One of them shrugged. "There are some men in the barn, and you see the ones working in the yard. Some of them might be interested in your snuff. You can warm up by the fire for a few minutes."

"Thank you kindly." Nicholas remounted Syllabub, saluted the two men, and started up the long path.

He headed directly for the barn, where he saw a small fire surrounded by a cluster of redcoats. Nicholas dismounted again when he reached the group around the fire. He greeted them and began unpacking his wares. The soldiers, bored and eager for any diversion, gathered around him with curiosity.

"Do ye have any rum?" asked a tall, unshaven soldier with a thin reddish beard in the same unusual accent Nicholas had noted before.

"We have plenty of rum," another objected. "I just want me a girl."

There was a round of laughter and coarse jesting. Nicholas grinned around at the circle.

"I have no rum nor girls either, in my bags, I'm sorry to say. But I did manage to pick up a couple of bottles of peach brandy in my travels." He displayed them to the curious cluster.

One portly soldier took the bottle in his hands and turned it around in a caressing gesture. "How much?"

Nicholas shrugged. "Two shillings."

"Two shillings!" The man sounded outraged, but he did not return the bottle.

Nicholas shrugged again. "'Tis fine peach brandy, made by one of the good wives of New Jersey. My grandmother used to make brandy just like this, and it was the sweetest nectar this side of heaven."

"One shilling," the man countered.

"Let me see." Nicholas turned over the remaining bottle in his hands. "Twenty pence, and you have yourself a bargain."

The soldier hesitated a second, shook the bottle, and then dug in his pocket for a coin. "I only have a shilling."

"I'll give you the eight pence," someone added, "if you'll give me half of that brandy."

Nicholas pocketed the money and turned to another soldier who wanted to buy snuff. He smiled and joked with the men as he conducted his trade, waiting for the best moment.

"I hope you fellows intend to stay around here for a while." He handed a third man a box of tobacco and pocketed the coins. "We're mighty grateful to have protection from those blamed rebels who are tearing the country apart."

"Those rebels can't stand against the King's army," one of the men boasted. "A gang of yokels with sticks and stones is all they are. No discipline, and deserting right and left from what I hear."

"They hate the bayonets." The portly soldier with the peach brandy waved the bottle at Nicholas as he spoke. "They'll fire their muskets at us, but as soon as we start a bayonet charge, they turn and scatter like a bunch of little scared rabbits."

"You can't blame them," Nicholas pointed out. "Look at their generals. Look at their officers. Not a real gentleman in the lot. Washington is the commander-in-chief of the army, and who is he? Just a planter from Virginia. The only war experience he had was in the French and Indian War, and he didn't even distinguish himself there."

The portly soldier laughed. "French and Indian War! These colonists have never fought in a real war. Now they're learning. Now they're finding out what it's like to face a real army."

Nicholas nodded as if granting the truth of his words. "Once you men get to Philadelphia, the rebellion is practically over, I hope."

"Aye." The soldier with the snuff dipped it and smeared it on his gums. "But that won't be till spring. I don't suppose General Howe wants to fight during the winter."

Nicholas nodded again, his voice very casual. "So you'll be staying this side of the river till spring. That's sensible, and I know the New Jersey folk will be glad of it."

A lean, fair-haired man was eying Nicholas with an expression he couldn't quite pinpoint. Was it suspicion? He went on, careful to keep his voice even, "Everyone around here is loyal to the King. Or rather, my family always has been. All my neighbors and friends. We just want this war over so life can get back to normal."

"Don't you worry, boy." The snuff man spit at the fire. "It'll be done with in no time. One more fight, come spring, we'll take Philadelphia, and all will be over. You'll see."

The fair man was silent, watching Nicholas. Nicholas turned and began packing his wares back in his bags. In spite of the cold he was beginning to sweat. Time to move on, without being too obvious. "I think I need to get going," he began, and then, over the back of Syllabub, he saw a man approach the group by the fire. Not a soldier; he wore no uniform. But the man looked exactly like one of his former neighbors from Philadelphia. Sam Wilcox. What was Wilcox doing here, in the middle of a British camp? What if he recognized Nicholas? He would know that Nicholas was no peddler; he might not have difficulty guessing his true mission.

Nicholas's heart nearly stopped. He swung up onto Syllabub, turning the horse to move away from the approaching figure. He could feel the eyes of the fair-haired soldier on his face.

Beside him someone called out, "When did you arrive, Hemmings?"

Involuntarily he glanced back at the new arrival. He had been mistaken. The face resembled Sam Wilcox, but belonged to a different man.

His heart slowed its mad hammering. He waved farewell to the redcoats around the fire and started down the long path to the road.

His breathing didn't return to normal until he was out on the road, heading away from the camp, and then he had leisure to consider what he had learned. No immediate plans to take Philadelphia. Perhaps he should have stayed longer; he might have learned more. That one soldier had panicked him by the way he was watching. And then that man with the uncanny resemblance to Sam Wilcox. Better safe than sorry, after all.

The sun was sinking low on the horizon and his stomach rumbled with hunger. He would need to find a place to spend the night, but before it got darker he would eat. He found a dry clearing on the side of the road, dismounted, and spread his blanket on the ground. He took the cornbread and half of the meat pie left from his noon meal and laid them on the blanket. He hesitated, then pulled the Bible from his bag. It was the Bible his sister Lavinia had thrust into his hands before he left home, and he had kept it as a memento of his family. He settled on his blanket to enjoy his meal, and as he did he thought of the thousands of men in the army who had not tasted such food in weeks.

Lord, thank you for this food...and for getting me safely out of another British camp...

What was happening to him? He had never prayed so much in his life. But he had never been so lonely and frightened and desperate, either. He knew he could die any day, and he knew he was not ready to meet God. And in spite of his anger and rebellion against God, he couldn't completely disbelieve in him.

He flipped the Bible open in the middle and his eyes slid over the page. *The Lord is merciful and gracious, slow to anger, and plenteous in mercy...For as the heaven is high above the earth, so great is his mercy toward them that fear him. As far as the east is from the west, so far hath he removed our transgressions from us. Like as a father pitieth his children, so the Lord pitieth them that fear him.*

His eyes fixed on the last sentence. Phoebe's words came back to him: "God accepts you, he loves you, even if your father doesn't."

Was it true? Could Phoebe be right? In his anger at his father, had he mistakenly rejected God's love as well? He wanted to believe, but how could he know?

For a long moment he lay on the blanket with his eyes closed, not actually praying, but thinking, remembering, trying to understand. Finally the chill winter wind roused him and he rose to remount Syllabub.

Lord Stirling had told him to return to the army before Christmas. Perhaps it was time. Perhaps he could find a way to get to Philadelphia and see Phoebe again. He wanted to see Phoebe, to talk to her, to remind her he was still alive. He felt a strange ache inside him that he could not completely define.

ஐ ᘓ

A week before Christmas Nicholas appeared at the Fuller home to share their dinner, although he had to rejoin his commander by nightfall, he said. His news of the army was no more sanguine than what they had heard from other sources, although it seemed to Phoebe he tried to steer the conversation in other directions. The optimism and enthusiasm of the summer months, the rapture that had accompanied the Declaration of Independence, had evaporated with the bloodbath of Brooklyn Heights, the mortification of the loss of Fort Washington, and this wretched retreat to the Delaware. Phoebe overheard him telling her father in a low voice that Washington himself had said "the game is pretty near up," and that one more defeat would spell the end of the rebel cause.

He joined Phoebe after dinner as she was washing the dishes in the kitchen and offered to wipe them for her. Phoebe tossed him the towel with a look of surprise.

"We're used to doing all sorts of tasks in the army," he informed her loftily. "We have to get along without women, you understand."

"Somehow I doubt you do many dishes in the army," Phoebe laughed.

"We don't usually have dishes. We're lucky whenever we have food."

"Which is why you use any pretext to come into the city and get a decent meal."

"Aye," he grinned, "And to catch a glimpse of the fair sex."

She dipped a soapy bowl into the tepid rinse water and handed it to him. "So you still haven't learned to get along without women?"

"We get along," he told her, "but 'tis mighty uncomfortable."

There was a brief pause.

"Is that Quincy fellow still coming around bothering you?" he asked.

Phoebe smiled into the dishwater and shrugged. "He was here once last week."

"My cousin was in a situation like yours once." He set down the bowl and picked up another. "Her parents wanted her to marry one fellow, but she preferred someone else."

Phoebe wanted to ask why he would think she preferred someone else, but decided against it. She wasn't sure she wanted to hear the answer. "What did your cousin do?"

"She got a child," Nicholas said, "then her parents let her marry who she wanted."

Phoebe shot him an indignant glare. "You would think of something so vulgar!"

"'Twasn't my idea!" he returned with a grin. "You asked what my cousin did; I never suggested you should follow in her footsteps."

"I wouldn't dream of it," she told him contemptuously, adding as an afterthought, "besides, I'd more likely be left with no husband at all."

"Phoebe!" he exclaimed, "how can you say—" He broke off, biting his lip and looking annoyed. He seemed to realize she was referring to him, although she hadn't quite said so.

Phoebe turned away to hide a smile, secretly pleased by his response. She sometimes suspected Nicholas was not nearly as hard and cynical as he liked to pretend.

She scrubbed at a stubborn spot on the bowl she held. "What are your plans, Nicholas? Do you plan to leave the army at the end of the year?"

"Nay," he replied simply. "I will stay with Washington until he surrenders, or until I am killed or wounded, whichever comes first."

At the gravity of his words Phoebe turned to study his face as she handed him the bowl. "So you do not hold out hope for victory?"

He hesitated, turning the bowl over in his hands and wiping it carefully. "It does not look well," he said finally.

Phoebe's heart dropped, although she was not totally surprised. For Nicholas, usually so sanguine and confident, to sound so hopeless meant the army's situation was grim indeed. And coupled with her fear for the army and their political cause was also concern for her family's personal safety. "Do you think the British plan to cross the river and occupy Philadelphia, as people are saying?"

"From what I have observed, they intend to stay in New Jersey throughout the winter. I hope it is true."

"What you have observed? What do you mean?"

He hesitated, glancing up and down for a moment, then around the room, as if looking for listening ears. "Do you want to know where I have been the last two weeks?" He lowered his voice. "I have been wandering through New Jersey, selling tobacco and talking Tory to the British and Hessian troops." He grinned mischievously. "For someone with a Tory family like mine, it comes naturally."

Phoebe dropped the bowl she was washing back into the water and turned to grasp his sleeve, her face horrified. "You mean you were *spying*? Oh, Nicholas, no! If they catch you, they'll hang you!"

His smile vanished, replaced by a grim expression. "Well I know it. Just like they hanged that poor devil in New York, Nathan Hale. I think about that fellow every night. But the army has learned something about spying since then. We don't carry any papers, so they aren't likely to be able to prove anything against us. And Washington needs to know what the enemy is up to."

His words gave scant comfort to Phoebe. She remembered Mr. Kirby saying that spying was the most dangerous job in the army, that experienced soldiers with little fear of battle shrank at the prospect of being caught up and hanged as a spy. And Nicholas was daily putting his head in a noose!

Suddenly he dropped his towel and swung her toward him, grasping her shoulders in his two hands. He searched her face intently. "Listen, Phoebe, you mustn't tell anyone about this, do you understand? Not even your own family. Especially your family. Do you promise?"

She nodded, frightened by his tone.

"I shouldn't have told you, I shouldn't have told anyone, but I wanted someone to know, in case I don't come back—" he hesitated and looked away, swallowing hard, "would you tell my mother?"

She nodded again, her throat too tight for words. Nicholas released her and picked up the towel again.

"So you are going back there again?" she whispered.

"I don't know. If a battle is planned soon, I might be kept with the army."

Phoebe did not know whether to be consoled by that possibility or not. She went to the back door and threw out the dirty tepid water, and then began to stack the clean bowls and replace them in the cupboard.

"I've been thinking about what you told me," Nicholas said suddenly.

Phoebe glanced at him over her shoulder. "What did I tell you?"

Nicholas was staring down at his hands, picking at his fingernails. "You said my father isn't God, and God accepts me even if my father doesn't."

Phoebe remembered. It had seemed like a weak unconvincing comment at the time. "Aye, 'tis true."

"I want to believe it," Nicholas said in a low voice. "For so long I have seen God as the enemy, but perhaps I was wrong."

"God isn't your enemy, Nicholas," Phoebe said earnestly.

He smiled crookedly. "I have read the Bible, too. Those nights across the river, all alone, I've read the Bible my sister gave me before I left."

Phoebe tried to think of some profound response, and failed. "I'm pleased."

He shrugged, and she had the feeling that he was trying to make light of a situation that affected him deeply. "I reckon that if I'm going to be hanged, I'd better prepare to meet my Maker."

"Oh, Nicholas!" Phoebe felt tears sting her eyes, and then bit her lip to gain self- control. "Any of us could meet our Maker at any time, you know."

He came to face her, once more laying his hands on her shoulders, squeezing gently. "Will you pray for me?" he whispered.

She met his gaze then, his sparkling hazel gaze which was now uncharacteristically solemn. "I always do, Nicholas," she said softly, "and I won't stop until you are safe at home for good. In every way."

80 03

"Only two more weeks till George is home to stay!" Sarah declared. The family was gathered around the table after dinner the day following Nicholas's visit, their father glancing through his newspaper while the women cleared the table. "I will be *so* relieved to have him safe and sound and not have to worry anymore."

Sally clapped her hands. "George is coming home?"

"His term of enlistment expires at the end of the year," her mother explained.

"But he can't come home then!" Phoebe swung around to face her mother. "If no one reenlists, the army will disintegrate!"

Her mother turned on her in fury. "It is already disintegrating, don't you understand? The war is over! I just want George safely home!"

Phoebe fell silent, as she always did in the face of her mother's wrath. A gust of wind blew down the chimney and into the kitchen, along with smoke and sparks from the fire. Phoebe coughed and fanned the air before her face, then carried a fresh log to the fireplace and laid it on top of the sputtering embers, her eyes smarting from the smoke.

Her father said, "I have something here that you might interest you, Phoebe."

Phoebe joined him at the table and followed where his finger was pointing at the newspaper. He was reading in the *Pennsylvania Journal* an article by Thomas Paine, whose *Common Sense* had earlier in the year fanned the flames of revolution. She scanned the words.

> These are the times that try men's souls. The summer soldier and the sunshine patriot will, in this crisis, shrink from the service of his country, but he that stands it now, deserves the love and thanks of man and woman.

"That's what I mean!" Phoebe exclaimed. "I worry about George too, but I don't want George to be a summer soldier or a sunshine patriot; I want him to stand by the cause even though it seems to be the darkest day."

Her mother suddenly clapped a hand to her mouth and ran out of the room, nearly in tears. Phoebe watched her in astonishment, then turned to her father in helpless bewilderment.

Her father smiled his gentle, sad smile. "Be patient with your mother, Phoebe. This is all new to her, and 'tis hard for her to see one of her children in danger. It is hard for her to let go."

Quick tears stung Phoebe's eyes. "I don't want George to die either!"

"Of course not." Her father patted her shoulder. "But you are able to stay focused on the larger picture, while your mother can only see what is directly before her. Be patient with her, Phoebe. Perhaps she will understand in the end."

ജ Chapter Nine beta

Christmas Eve awoke cold and overcast, with the damp scent of snow or sleet in the air. Sarah and her daughters began working on the feast for the next day, dutifully preparing for their guests, although Phoebe could not remember such a gloomy holiday in her life. Sarah wondered aloud if George would have any celebration with the army at all, and Phoebe, recalling Nicholas's comments about the state of the army, wondered if he would even have a real meal. Did her brother even have shoes and blankets in this bitter weather to keep the cold away? And Nicholas—however much she tried to focus on her own brother, she couldn't help remember that he might even now be spying for the army in the British camps of New Jersey. Although perhaps warmer and better clothed, his situation would be far more dangerous.

"I hope you don't object, Mother," Alice said as she cut into the pumpkin that would make their pie, "but I invited Edmund to our dinner tomorrow, and he agreed to come."

Sarah brightened at the news. Phoebe's courtship might be sputtering, but Alice's was blazing warmer than ever, and Phoebe knew that her mother had high hopes of a wedding in the near future. A wedding—and grandchildren. It was something for her to look forward to, and it comforted her to think Edmund had no interest in the war.

"Of course Edmund is always welcome," Sarah replied, and then was interrupted by the opening of the front door and her husband's and sons' heavy footsteps and voices. "Sarah! Girls!" their father called.

"Come see your Christmas surprise!"

The surprise was a new Franklin stove, named for its inventor and known to be far more efficient in heating homes than the huge, open, drafty fireplaces which were used for both warmth and cooking. Richard Fuller and the boys lugged it into the parlor in pieces, where they began to assemble it with clangs and bangs.

"If the rest of the winter is as cold as this month has been, we'll need something to warm this house," Richard said. "I hope to get it all ready to use before tomorrow when our guests arrive."

So the next day the stove was set up in a corner of the parlor and consuming its first load of wood as the family gathered around the table for Christmas dinner. The aroma of roasted goose filled the room, and the table was laden with pewter and silver and bowls of turnips, succotash, cranberries, and a plum pudding. Phoebe carefully carried a large bowl of punch in from the kitchen and set it on the sideboard.

"We have much to be thankful for," Richard Fuller said as the room fell silent, but Phoebe thought she saw his lips tremble a bit. He asked the blessing on the food, asking for God's protection and provision for the army and especially for their own loved ones who were fighting, and for a moment silence reigned when he finished. Then the bowls and platters began to circle the table and cheerful chatter filled the room as the guests and family filled their plates.

"We received a letter just last week from our friends, the Palmers, in New York," Phoebe's aunt commented as she refilled her plate for the second time with goose and stuffing. She was a plump, cheerful, talkative woman, one of Phoebe's favorite relatives, although she was only related to the Fullers by marriage. "What an experience they are having with all those British soldiers in the city, and the Tories running everything. We might have the same condition here, if Washington's army doesn't stop the British soon."

"Washington's army is in no condition to stop anyone," her husband observed gloomily.

"Did you give Phoebe her letter, Papa?" Kit asked.

Phoebe looked up from her plate, a spoonful of turnips halfway to her mouth. "A letter? For me?"

"The letter! Gracious, I did indeed forget!" her father exclaimed. "I picked it up yesterday when we fetched the stove home, and with all the activity here, completely forgot to give it to you." He rose and crossed to his desk, then brought a letter to Phoebe. "Merry Christmas!"

Surprised, Phoebe examined the handwriting, expecting it to be Lavinia's, for she had written to her friend several weeks before. But the writing was different, although she had, she thought, seen it once. Suddenly she broke the seal and scanned the bottom of the sheet for the signature with its large scrawling flourish.

"It is from Nicholas," she breathed in amazement.

Her younger brothers snickered before their father stopped them with a glance, but Phoebe was oblivious. Nicholas had written to her! Why would he write her a letter? She could scarcely bear to wait to read it, and was torn between a desire for privacy and desperation to know its contents immediately. It would be rude to leave the table while everyone was eating, and so she restrained her impatience, although she barely heard the conversation that swirled around her.

As soon as Martha began to clear the table Phoebe rose as if to help her, and with her letter in her pocket retreated to her bedroom to read in quiet. As she opened the letter she admired Nicholas's handwriting: neat and scholarly, yet very masculine.

My dear Phoebe,

I have an opportunity to send a letter by courier to Philadelphia this afternoon, and therefore will try to write a few hasty lines. I sense we will be going into battle soon, and I may not have the opportunity to write again; for this reason I feel the urgency to do so now, however disorganized my communication may be. I know no plans of the impending battle, and could not impart them if I did; however, I sense that Washington will not be satisfied without taking a stand before the end of the year. I believe you comprehend the desperate situation of the army.

I told you last week I had been reading the Bible that my sister gave me. I cannot well explain the new spiritual hunger I have experienced. Perhaps it is the result of facing death daily, or the influence of godly friends such as yourself. For several weeks at least, or even months, I have felt God calling me, but have scarcely known how to respond. Phrases from my reading, comments that you have made, memories of my mother—all of these have played repeatedly through my mind. I now believe God has been using them to reach me.

Two days ago I was reading the story of the lost sheep, which I had certainly heard before, but this time I knew the lost sheep was myself, and that God was leaving his ninety-nine sheep in the wilderness to find me. And then I read about the lost son whose father welcomed him home in the end, and God met me. I can offer no better explanation than that, but I felt God was speaking to me, saying "I am the Father who is welcoming you home, even if your earthly father never does."

Phoebe, I have experienced such peace since that night, joy and comfort even in the midst of these dreadful circumstances. I do not know if I will return from this next battle; it is very possible I will not, and for this reason I wanted you to know that I have found peace with God before my death. Please, if I don't return, I ask you to write to my mother. I know this news will be a great comfort to her. I hope my father will be glad to hear it as well.

Phoebe read the letter through once, so rapidly that she barely comprehended the whole meaning, but her heart flooded with joy and gratitude as she realized what Nicholas was communicating to her. *Thank you, Lord,* she breathed. *Even if I never see him again, I'm so thankful that Nicholas has found peace with you.*

She was in the middle of reading a second time when Alice's voice came from the foot of the stairs.

"Phoebe, are you up there? Mother says to hurry down and help with the dishes."

Phoebe dropped the letter on the bed and hurried below, a singing in her heart. Alice and Sally had already cleared most of the dishes while the men sat and talked around the table. Phoebe carried the coffeepot into the parlor and refilled her uncle's cup, then her father's.

She noticed that Edmund's place was empty.

"Where is Edmund?" she asked her father.

Her father glanced up. "He left the table a minute ago. He didn't say where he was going."

Phoebe refilled his cup anyway. Perhaps Edmund had gone to the kitchen to speak to Alice. She returned to the kitchen to help serve the pumpkin and mincemeat pies.

Her aunt looked up with a smile from the table where she was cutting the pies, her eyes bright with curiosity. "There you are, Phoebe! Did you read your letter? Who is this Nicholas who is writing to you?"

"He's—he's an old friend of the family." Phoebe tried to sound casual, although she knew her eyes were sparkling. "He's serving in the army with Washington."

Her aunt shook her head at that piece of information. "A beau of yours?"

"Nay." Phoebe knew she was blushing, although she shook her head firmly. "He used to be our neighbor and he visits whenever he is in town. He rides courier and comes into the city rather often."

"But he wrote to you, not to your parents or Alice," her aunt persisted, still with a twinkle in her eye.

Phoebe shrugged, trying not to smile. "I'm not certain why he did that, except that we have gotten to be friends."

Her aunt still wore that knowing look, but there was nothing more Phoebe could do to convince her. If only her aunt were right! If only Phoebe could say, "Aye, Nicholas is my beau, we've been courting for several months now." She felt a surge of longing at the image. But she knew the real reason Nicholas had written to her was that she was the closest link he had to his family, and the only one who understood how matters stood between him and his parents.

"Here, Phoebe, this spinning wheel is in my way." Sarah pushed it aside as she bustled up to the table where Phoebe and her aunt were working. "Move it into the hall, will you please? That will give us more room in here."

Phoebe opened the door to the hall and dragged the spinning wheel out of the kitchen and into the room where the other household equipment was kept. The hall was empty, but as she started back to the kitchen, she heard footsteps on the staircase and then saw Edmund emerge at the foot of it. He gave her one brief startled glance and disappeared into the parlor where the family was eating.

Phoebe stared after him, perplexed. Edmund had gone upstairs! Why would he do that? There was nothing upstairs to interest him, only the two bedrooms where the children slept. And Alice was in the kitchen; he couldn't have been talking to her up there. How odd!

There was probably some simple explanation. On the other hand, he had seemed startled at the sight of Phoebe, as if she had caught him in the act of something dishonest. Why would he go sneaking around their bedrooms? Was he trying to steal something that belonged to Alice? She had heard of men who took their sweethearts' gloves and handkerchiefs and kept them as love tokens. But that seemed like a silly thing for Edmund to do. He had never seemed like the sentimental type to her. Alice would certainly be astonished and perhaps offended if she learned he had resorted to such subterfuge.

With curiosity but no clear idea of what she expected to find, Phoebe climbed the stairs to her bedroom and glanced around. The chest where the girls kept their clothes was still closed. She went to open it, to see if anything was missing, although she doubted it. But with her hand on the clasp she glanced around the room and her eyes fell on the quilt that covered their bed.

Her letter! It was gone!

She went to the bed, but nothing was there. Perhaps it had fallen on the floor. She searched the floor around the bed, pulled out Sally's trundle bed, and got down on her hands and knees to search under the bed. She found an old hair ribbon and two buttons, but no letter.

She groped in her pocket. Perhaps she had put it in there and forgotten. Her pocket was empty.

Edmund took my letter! The thought was incredible, but there it was. *I left the letter here, he came up, and now it is gone!*

Was she mad? Was she imagining things? Why on earth would Edmund want a letter from Nicholas? Why would he care about that? It made no sense.

And then she remembered the letter Nicholas had copied that had vanished from the desk the night when Edmund was visiting. A letter from his commander, Nicholas had told her. Information about the war. Could all these disappearing letters possibly be a coincidence?

She felt cold inside, and her breath began to come fast. What had Nicholas written about the army? Something about a battle before the end of the year, that Washington intended to take a stand. Had he given any other particulars? Any details? She couldn't remember.

She ran down the steps two at a time, almost ripping her best petticoat. The rest of the family was seated around the table in the parlor eating pie and drinking coffee, but Edmund was missing. She ran to the kitchen where she found Alice giving instructions to the servant.

"Where's Edmund?" she demanded, grabbing her sister's arm.

Alice looked up, surprised at her breathless agitation. "He just left. He came in here a moment ago and told me he needed to go home early. His parents are expecting guests today and wanted him to be there to meet them."

"He just told you this now? He didn't mention it earlier?"

"He didn't, actually. I was surprised he had to leave so early, because he hadn't told me so before."

Phoebe hesitated, but the coincidence was too great. "Edmund took my letter."

"Your letter? What do you mean?"

"The letter from Nicholas. I left the letter on our bed upstairs. I saw him coming down from the bedrooms, so I went up, and the letter was gone."

Alice's face darkened. "Don't be absurd, Phoebe. Why would Edmund care about a letter from Nicholas?"

"It came from the army! He probably thought it contained military information."

A sudden look of fear crossed Alice's face, and when she spoke her voice was sharp with anger. "What are you saying, Phoebe? Edmund is no spy! He cares nothing about politics!"

"How do you know, Alice? I saw him at the State House last July, when they were reading the Declaration! And you've heard the things he's said, about how foolish we are to try to fight the King's army."

"And so? You were there that day as well, but you are no spy!"

Phoebe suddenly snatched her cloak from its peg on the wall. "I have to find him. I have to stop him."

Alice grabbed her arm, and Phoebe had never seen her sister look so angry or so afraid. "Are you mad, Phoebe? Do you know how much trouble you can cause by making wild accusations? Let me talk to Edmund first. There's probably some simple explanation for all this. Edmund wouldn't do anything so foolish or dangerous."

Phoebe hesitated, for she had never opposed Alice in her life. But something, instinct or intuition, told her that this time she was right and Alice was wrong.

"I have to go." She shook off her sister's hand and dashed out the door.

There was no sign of Edmund on the street. How much time had he gained on her? Five, ten minutes? No more than that. Where should she go first to look for him? She had no idea. She knew where he lived, and there was always a possibility that he had gone home, just as he had told Alice. It was the only place she could think of to look.

She started down the street at a trot, the iciness of the winter air striking her face and freezing her breath as she ran. She tasted snow in the air and smelled it in the low-hanging clouds. In her haste she had forgotten her hood and mittens, and she dug her hands into her pockets for warmth. She needed to formulate a plan before she arrived at Edmund's house. Could she just walk up to him and say, "Edmund, my letter is missing. Did you take it?" Edmund would surely never admit to such a theft. She would feel foolish asking the question. On the other hand, such a move would at least make him aware she suspected him. Perhaps he would hesitate to pass the letter on to anyone if he knew he had aroused suspicion.

She reached the house before deciding for sure on a plan. Slowing her pace, she approached the door, her heart pounding, as possible approaches swirled through her mind. What could she possibly say? "Edmund, I know you're a spy, and I'll report you if you don't return my letter to me"? She would never be able to say such a thing. She felt a thickness in her throat made it impossible to swallow.

She knocked on the door and a moment later heard footsteps within. Edmund's mother, a rail-thin woman in a checkered apron, her graying hair tucked under her mobcap, opened the door.

"Phoebe!" The woman held the door open for her. "Come in! What are you doing here?"

"Good day, Mrs. Ingram." Phoebe stepped into the hall and glanced around, trying to breathe normally. "I'm looking for Edmund."

"Edmund? Goodness, child, Edmund isn't here. Isn't he at your house? He told me Alice had invited him for Christmas dinner. That she wanted him to meet your relatives who were coming to visit."

Phoebe nodded, still panting. "Aye, he was there. But he left a few minutes ago. He said you were having company, and wanted him to come home early."

Mrs. Ingram shook her head, her expression puzzled. "Why would Edmund say something like that? We don't have any company here today. I assumed he would be spending the whole evening at your house."

Phoebe felt her heart plummet. For a moment she was speechless with dismay.

"I don't know where to look for him now," she said finally.

"Goodness, I don't know either. Why would Edmund make up a story like that? All I can imagine is he wanted to meet some other friends and was afraid your sister would disapprove. He may be at a tavern with his good friend, Harry Hastings."

Phoebe took a deep breath, trying to think. "Do you know what tavern he usually visits?"

The woman frowned. "Let me think. There is one called the Blue Bell, but I don't know exactly where it is located. I'm sorry, Phoebe. Is this a crisis? Has something happened to Alice, or your parents?"

"Nay." Phoebe managed a smile. "'Tis nothing like that. My family is well. I wanted to ask Edmund a question, but I'm sure I'll have another opportunity the next time he comes to call."

"I'll tell Edmund you were looking for him." Mrs. Ingram clearly wanted to be helpful.

"You needn't trouble yourself. I'll talk to him later." Phoebe was already opening the door. "Thank you."

Out on the street she looked right and left. Which direction was the Blue Bell tavern? There were so many taverns in Philadelphia. Was it near Market Street? She started in that direction, praying it was the one she remembered. The wind bit into her face and whistled in her ears. Frantically she scanned each tavern sign she passed, ignoring the curious glances and snide remarks from some young men who had imbibed too much Christmas cheer.

Finally, after walking the cobbled streets for what seemed like several miles, she spotted a tavern with a picture of a blue bell hanging in front, and she opened the door. Warmth enveloped her and the scent of roast pork and ale met her nostrils. Inside the door she paused to catch her breath and let her eyes adjust to the gloom. Her eyes scanned the faces at the tables.

"Welcome, mistress. Are you looking for someone perhaps?"

Phoebe looked up to see a tall balding man who appeared to be the tavern owner.

"I was wondering—" she paused to catch her breath, "does a man named Edmund Ingram ever come to this tavern?"

"Aye, Ingram, certainly he does. I know him well. Several times a week at least."

Phoebe nodded eagerly, turning once again to search the faces. "Is he here now, by any chance?"

"He was here, I believe," the man told her. "Perhaps an hour ago, but he didn't stay."

Phoebe's heart fell. "He—he didn't say where he was going, did he?"

She saw a slight, knowing smile at the corners of the man's mouth, and suddenly blushed at the situation she found herself in. But it didn't matter what this man thought of her. Nothing mattered but finding Edmund and her letter.

"Nay, I fear not."

Dejected, Phoebe turned to the door. Once on the street, she started slowly for home. She had no idea where Edmund might have gone. Probably it didn't matter now anyway. Edmund had had ample time to read her letter and pass whatever information it contained to whomever he wanted.

She was halfway home, passing the street that led to the Kirby home, when another idea struck her. She turned and headed to the Kirbys'.

ও ଓ

"Do you really think Edmund Ingram is passing information to the British?" Mr. Kirby asked fifteen minutes later after Phoebe had explained her fears to him.

"I don't know," Phoebe said, "and I would hate to accuse someone falsely. But it is so strange the way he lied to my sister about going home when he was really going to that tavern. And it is even stranger the way letters keep disappearing when he is visiting, and always letters connected with the army. Oh, Mr. Kirby, I am so frightened that news of Washington's plans will reach the British, and the army will be captured and it will be all my fault."

Mr. Kirby mused for a moment in silence, turning all this information over in his mind. "I will share your worries with the Council of Public Safety, and they will decide whether Ingram is actually a threat," he said finally. "As for this particular battle your friend mentioned in the letter, without knowing his contacts it may be impossible to stop him. Sometimes, Phoebe, there is nothing we can do but pray."

"Then I will certainly do that, and most fervently," Phoebe said.

☙ Chapter Ten ❧

In spite of the warmth of the new Franklin stove, the air was chilly between the Fuller sisters the next day. Alice awoke and dressed in silence, then avoided Phoebe during their morning activities, and Phoebe, finding her sister so uncommunicative, decided against relating her conversation with Mr. Kirby. She knew Alice would not be pleased to hear that her sister's suspicions were being reported to the Council of Public Safety. Phoebe answered her mother's inquiries about her disappearance the night before as vaguely as possible. No reason to alarm her mother unnecessarily, especially since she felt sure her mother would agree with Alice.

Late in the afternoon when Alice and her mother left to visit a sick church member and carry a kettle of soup to the family, Phoebe chose to stay at home. She was a bit surprised that as yet Alice had not told her mother about their altercation, and guessed Alice herself was not completely convinced of Edmund's innocence, or she would have enlisted her mother's support. Either way, there was nothing she could do now but pray.

She took advantage of her mother's absence to carry a book into the parlor, but for once found it impossible to lose herself in the story. Her mind kept returning to the events of the day before, to Nicholas's letter, and to the battle the dying army would be fighting, perhaps at that very moment.

Did I do wrong, Lord? she asked for the tenth time that day. *I don't want to hurt Edmund, of course, but I also don't want Edmund to hurt the army. How confusing loyalty can be in such a situation! Lord, please protect the army as they go into battle, and if it is your will, don't let our cause for independence be completely destroyed. And please protect Nicholas and George. And oh, Lord, I am so thankful that Nicholas knows you now and has found peace with you, even if he is killed. But please, please don't let him be killed!*

She tried not to think beyond that. She was, of course, highly gratified that Nicholas had chosen to share his experience with her, but she couldn't and wouldn't read any more into it. For Nicholas's sake, not her own, she was happy he knew the Lord.

She heard a clatter on the street in front of the house, and rose to look out of the front window. An unfamiliar carriage was stopped in front of the Fuller house. She heard a knock on the door and Martha's footsteps as she hurried to open it.

A moment later the parlor door opened and Lavinia Teasdale entered, followed by her mother and sister Charlotte.

"Lavinia!" Phoebe cried, surprised beyond words. She ran to embrace her friend, and was doubly surprised to receive a second embrace from Mrs. Teasdale. "How wonderful of you to come and call!"

"We are in town for Christmas, visiting my grandparents," Lavinia explained. "I told my mother we could not leave without seeing you once again."

Phoebe bade them all be seated, and called to Martha to bring some coffee and cakes. As she took the guests' cloaks, she admired their lovely silk gowns in violet, turquoise, and yellow, and wished she were wearing something equally fine. The Teasdales were certainly doing well for themselves, and she recalled Alice's opinion that Nicholas was beyond their reach. For the next five minutes the four women exchanged the happy chatter of old friends reunited after a long separation.

"I am so sorry my mother and Alice are gone right now," Phoebe said as she explained their errand. "I certainly expect them to return soon."

"I am glad *you* are at home," Lavinia returned. "You are the one we most wanted to see."

Mrs. Teasdale hesitated a moment, and Phoebe suddenly realized that to her, this visit was more than just a call on an old acquaintance. "Phoebe, have you actually seen Nicholas lately?" Her eyes, pleading, were fixed on the girl's face.

"I saw him one week ago, and I received a letter from him just yesterday." Phoebe clasped her hands together and proceeded to relate from memory the details of the letter. His mother's face grew brighter as she spoke, and by the end the lady was blinking back tears.

"Oh, I am so thankful!" Mrs. Teasdale wiped her eyes with her handkerchief. "It is what I have longed to hear. If only he might be reconciled with his father, I would have nothing to wish for, but I suppose that will be impossible before we leave."

Phoebe glanced at Lavinia with a question in her eyes. Lavinia said hesitantly, "You see, we will be leaving for England in the next few weeks. We are waiting for my father to conclude his business here, and then we will stay in England until this rebellion is over."

"Then I won't see you again," Phoebe said slowly.

"Nay, but you must write to us." Mrs. Teasdale leaned toward her. "Oh, Phoebe, you are a good girl, and I know you must be a wholesome influence on Nicholas. If you could kindly look out for him while we are gone, I would be so terribly grateful."

Phoebe patted the weeping woman's hand. "I will do whatever I can," she said sincerely. "I love him too."

The words slipped out of her mouth before she had a chance to weigh them, and instantly she could have bitten her tongue. But Nicholas's mother did not appear shocked or disapproving.

"I am happy to hear it." She squeezed the girl's hand. "And I hope he loves you too. I believe he must, to have written you such a letter, although he may not realize it himself."

For a moment the four of them sat in silence as Mrs. Teasdale wiped her eyes and the two sisters exchanged glances. As Phoebe tried to swallow her embarrassment at her faux pas she caught a glimpse of a horse and rider passing by in the street just outside the window. Something about the size and color of the horse, or perhaps the figure of the rider, made her suddenly rise and move to the passage outside the parlor, opening the front door just in time to see Nicholas swing down from Syllabub and stumble toward the house. He did not even pause or greet her on the threshold, but fell into the passage and caught her in his arms, his own shaking as he clutched her.

"Oh, Phoebe," he gasped, "I have been to hell and back, and it was cold, not hot like they say. I have never been so cold in my life."

He was certainly cold in her arms, his coat filthy and caked with snow and mud, his face covered with several days' growth of stubble. Phoebe was so startled by both his words and his embrace that it was a moment before she could find her voice to stammer, "Nicholas—where have you been?"

He straightened then and partially released her, and when she was able to look in his face she saw, in spite of his shivering exhaustion, that his eyes were dancing with excitement.

"We've been to Trenton!" he exclaimed, "and oh, Phoebe, it was marvelous! We captured the entire Hessian command!"

For a moment Phoebe was sure he was joking. "Impossible!" she cried. "What are you talking about?"

Nicholas hugged her again, and this time nearly lifted her off her feet. "'Tis true!" he laughed, "and it was beautiful! We surprised the Hessians in the morning, when they had just gone back to bed after roll call, and Colonel Rall had even sent in the sentries because of the cold! The timing was perfect, simply perfect, beyond what any general could have planned, and could only have been the work of divine Providence." He stopped suddenly, and Phoebe felt his arms go limp. She turned and saw that his mother was standing in the parlor door. Nicholas had just seen her.

"Mother," he whispered, and then he was in her arms and she was crying against his shoulder.

"Mother, Mother, don't cry," he managed, although his own voice to Phoebe sounded suspiciously choked.

"God is so good," she sobbed. "I prayed I would be able to see you once more before we left, but I truly didn't believe it would be possible."

Phoebe swallowed hard at the sight of them together and then slipped back into the parlor to leave them alone. Lavinia and Charlotte had run to the front door behind their mother and Phoebe could hear them all talking at once. But two minutes later Nicholas entered the parlor with his mother and sisters still clinging to him. They found seats and talked hard, making up for eighteen months in their brief visit. Lavinia and Charlotte related the news of all their friends and relatives, everything important that had occurred in the last year and a half, and then Nicholas shared his experiences in the army, dwelling in particular detail on the victory that very day in Trenton. Nearly an hour passed as they talked, and when Phoebe glanced out the window she was surprised to find the eastern sky had faded to dusk.

"I always believed it was wrong for King George to send mercenaries to wage war against his own subjects," his mother sighed when Nicholas had finished relating his story. "Oh, this war is so dreadful. But my dear, it heartens me to see you so fine and manly and honest and well-grown. I believe this last year has been the making of you, for all its difficulties." And then, without changing her tone in the least, she added, "Now if you promise you will marry Phoebe when you can find the time, I will not ask any more."

Phoebe started and felt her face grow hot in horrified embarrassment, but when she met Nicholas's gaze across his mother's head, she saw that he was laughing.

"Phoebe might have something to say to the matter, Mother," he returned with a grin. "Why, the last I heard she was being courted by a charming, personable young fellow named Miles Quincy. Perhaps I should carry her off to our country estate and hold her prisoner there until she accepts me."

Mrs. Teasdale glanced uncertainly from the young lady's scarlet countenance to her irrepressible son. "Nonsense!" she exclaimed. "You can certainly charm her with no difficulty."

"Not always," Nicholas replied with a twinkle. Phoebe remembered the hot day in August that they had spent together at the fair, and felt her face grow warmer.

The conversation was interrupted by the entrance of Alice and her mother, returning from their visit. After exchanging pleasantries with her old friend, Mrs. Teasdale reluctantly told her children it was time to depart. She embraced her son, shedding tears once more before taking leave. Phoebe slipped away to the kitchen to help put the evening meal on the table.

Ten minutes later supper was ready, but when the family gathered around the table Nicholas was missing. Phoebe called his name, and then, finding him nowhere below, climbed the stairs to her brothers' bedroom and peeked through the door that stood ajar.

Nicholas was sprawled out on George's bed, still fully dressed, and fast asleep.

೩ ೧೮

"I reckon no one will call to replace Washington now," Phoebe said.

Nicholas had slept through the entire night, much to his chagrin, and was spending a few moments alone with Phoebe after breakfast before heading back to rejoin his commander. Her mother, with a question in her raised eyebrows, had left them alone in the kitchen washing dishes while she and Alice started the rest of the daily housework.

"Aye, I'm sure of it. Washington has certainly redeemed himself this time, and this victory should silence most of his critics. Especially now that Charles Lee had been captured. Lee was a bit of a fool, and Washington has shown his genius."

"What do you really think, Nicholas?" Phoebe looked up from the pewter bowl she was scrubbing. "Was it Washington's genius, or simply brilliant luck?"

"Or God's providence," Nicholas returned with a smile. "I'm sure there was a bit of all of those in that victory. 'Twas a bold, daring plan, and no one but Washington would have found the ingenuity to try it, or have inspired his men to follow him. And his use of the artillery was certainly brilliant. But luck was on our side as well. Everything seemed to go wrong at the time—the crossing took longer than we expected, and we reached Trenton much later than planned, but even in the timing we were fortunate, for the soldiers had already gone back to bed. And did I tell you the oddest thing of all? The Hessians were completely surprised, and yet we found a note in Colonel Rall's pocket, after he died, warning of the attack."

Phoebe suddenly recalled the letter from Nicholas which had mysteriously disappeared on Christmas Day. "The Hessians were warned?" she asked slowly.

"Aye, but for some odd reason they did not taking the warning seriously. Perhaps the colonel forgot to read the letter, or perhaps he thought the weather was too bad for an attack or did not expect it the day after Christmas."

"I know how they *might* have been warned," Phoebe said slowly, and she proceeded to relate the incident with Edmund and the vanishing letter. She expected Nicholas to be shocked, horrified, or even angry, but to her surprise when she glanced up at him she saw him wearing an amused smile.

"So Ingram got his hands on that letter of mine, did he?" he chuckled. "Well, I give him credit; I never imagined he was so clever. Every other time I practically had to place the letter in his hands."

Phoebe dropped the clean knives back in the dirty dish water as she turned to stare at him. "Are you saying you *knew* Edmund was giving information to the British? How did you know? And you *gave* him letters?"

Nicholas was laughing softly, and he glanced down at Phoebe as if uncertain how much to say. "Do you remember that day that I met you at the State House in July?" He lowered his voice. "I was here on a special assignment, to learn as much as I could about the enemy spy system in Philadelphia. I was pretty sure Edmund Ingram was involved somehow, and that day when you told me he was courting Alice, I thought I had the perfect opportunity to find out more."

"So that's why you came home with me that day!" Phoebe cried, not sure whether to feel admiration for his cleverness or indignation at his duplicity.

Nicholas grinned again, a bit sheepishly this time. "I know you thought I wanted to court Alice, but in reality I was trying to find out what she knew about his activities."

"I don't believe she knew anything," Phoebe inserted.

He nodded, running the towel over the pitcher she handed him. "I came to the same conclusion myself after a number of visits. But then my commander suggested another way to make use of the connection, by spreading false information about the army to the enemy."

"That letter you dropped last August—" Phoebe remembered, "that was really intended for Edmund all along?"

Nicholas rubbed his newly shaved chin, his eyes twinkling. "Did he take the bait then? I never did find out what happened with that. Aye, the letter was full of all sorts of nonsense about the generals' plans, written out in Lord Stirling's own handwriting. The second letter I left out on your father's desk, just within Edmund's reach."

"Nicholas Teasdale!" In her distraction Phoebe dropped one pewter bowl against another with a clatter. "I never imagined you could be so sly and deceitful!"

"Why Phoebe, you should know me better than that!" Nicholas laughed. "But he outwitted me this last time. I was so anxious to get that final letter to you, I forgot it might fall into the wrong hands. Fortunately, I didn't include much real intelligence."

"I will never believe a word you say again," Phoebe declared, quite thunderstruck by the revelations of the last few minutes.

Nicholas was quiet for a moment, and when he spoke his tone was different, odd for him, almost shy and hesitant. He set down the bowl in his hands and reached for another. "You can believe everything in that letter, for I certainly meant every word I wrote, although perhaps I've squandered my credibility with you. I want to be a different person than I used to be, or perhaps I should say, I *am* a different person, if you will give me a chance to prove it."

"You needn't prove anything to me, Nicholas," Phoebe said, uncertain where the conversation was leading or how she should respond. "God knows your heart, and his opinion is the only one that matters."

"Aye, he *does* know my heart, but your opinion matters too, Phoebe. Perhaps my intentions toward you were not completely honorable when we first became acquainted. I can't change that now, of course; I can only hope to redeem myself by showing I won't try to take advantage of you again."

Remembering his glibness the night he kissed her, Phoebe was struck by the difference in his tone, his diffidence and humility. She was humbled by the fact that he seemed to care for her good opinion, but hesitated to presume too much, as his mother had done, and felt herself floundering for an answer. She dipped another bowl into the murky dishwater.

"I have forgiven you for that, Nicholas. I will always consider you a good friend."

"Aye," he agreed, "I think you are the first real woman friend that I have ever had. 'Tis a strange experience, actually."

Phoebe smiled weakly and tried to feel very happy that she and

Nicholas were good friends. It was all she had ever expected, after all. She handed him the last bowl and opened the back door to dispose of the dishwater. When she returned to the kitchen, Nicholas was putting on his coat.

"I need to return to the army," he told her. "I have been away too long."

"Aye. I hope Lord Stirling will not be angry with you."

Nicholas grinned. "I am in good favor with him because of my adventures in New Jersey. He gives me a great deal of freedom now. But I don't want to abuse it."

"Of course not." She hesitated. "Do you think you will go into battle again soon?"

"I do not know. But I have to be available for whatever he needs me for."

Phoebe followed him to the front door, a yearning in her heart that she ached to show him. "Please be very careful, Nicholas."

His hand was on the latch, but he turned around to give her another smile. "As careful as I can be in the middle of a war. And you be careful, too, Phoebe."

For a moment she had no idea what he could be talking about. "Me?"

"Aye, in resisting the advances of brave Miles Quincy."

"Oh, him!" Embarrassed, Phoebe shook her head with a gesture of dismissal. "Never fear. He's always a perfect gentleman."

"Aye, I'm sure he is, and you may tell him that you have a gallant brother who is ready to defend your honor if he ever forgets himself."

Phoebe managed another weak smile. "Do you mean George?"

"George, and myself as well. Two gallant brothers."

Phoebe bit her lip. "Of course. I'll tell him so."

Nicholas's face grew more serious. "Please pray for me."

"I always do."

He opened the door and with a blast of winter cold, was gone.

Phoebe closed the door behind him and retreated to her bedroom, curled up on her bed, and laid her face against the cool pillowcase. It had been wonderful to see Nicholas again, to see him reunited with his family, and to hear of the army's splendid victory. The way he had confided in her had warmed her. And most importantly, how wonderful to know he had made peace with God! But then he had dampened his final good-bye with the comment about being her brother. Was that really the way he saw her? He had kissed her back in the summer, but that clearly had meant nothing to him, as he was willing to admit now. He was a Christian now, and she could only assume that along with his dissolute habits he had also discarded any romantic interest he might once have had in her—or Alice, for that matter. Only she now realized his interest in Alice had been primarily to learn about Edmund's activities. So maybe he had never really been interested in either of them—except as a brother.

She lay on the bed on her back, staring at the rafters. *It could be worse. At least we are friends. A brother is not such a bad thing to have. And Lord, thank you for whatever role I've been able to play in bringing Nicholas back to You and his family.* She felt one tear roll down the side of her face and into the quilt, and she quickly wiped it away.

She heard her mother's footsteps approaching the stairs and then her mother's voice. "Phoebe! Are you up there? Hurry on down and help with this washing!"

With a sigh, Phoebe pushed herself off the bed and moved to do her mother's bidding.

ℰ Chapter Eleven ℂ

During the first week of January, word trickled into Philadelphia of a second victory over the enemy. Washington's men had confronted the British at Princeton and scattered them. The Fuller family heard nothing from either George or Nicholas during these days, but they were heartened by the reassurance that the colonists had won the most recent battles. Sarah, in particular, resigned herself to the conviction that George intended to enlist for another year and would not be safely home as she longed to see him. Indeed, the two recent victories, as minor as they were, seemed to breathe new life into the rebel cause. People stopped saying the rebellion was finished, and a new spirit of patriotism invaded the city.

But Phoebe soon found that in the midst of this change of fortune not everyone was happy. One day Alice received a note from Edmund's mother, asking her to come to call. When she returned from the visit she retreated to her bedroom and closed the door. In the hall beneath where the other women were working, they could hear her restless footsteps pacing the floor.

"What do you suppose is the matter with your sister?" Sarah looked up from the pewter she was polishing.

Phoebe shook her head. "I have no idea. Didn't she just come from the Ingrams? Do you suppose something is wrong with the family?"

Sarah frowned. After a moment of waiting for her daughter to reappear, she put down her polishing rag and went toward the stairs.

Phoebe heard her knock on the bedroom door, and a moment later heard muted voices from the bedroom above. An uneasy feeling settled between Phoebe's heart and her stomach.

A moment later her mother's voice reached her. "Phoebe! Come here, please."

Sally looked up from her sampler to give her sister a glance of concern. Phoebe set down the candlesticks she was cleaning and started up the stairs, her mind heavy with foreboding.

She found her mother and sister standing together by the bed. Tear streaks marked Alice's face, while her mother looked stern.

"Phoebe," Sarah said, "what have you done?"

Phoebe looked from one to the other. "I don't know. What has happened? What's wrong?"

Alice wiped her wet cheeks angrily with the back of her hand. "This is all your fault! All because of your needless meddling! All because of what you did on Christmas day! Do you know what's happened? Edmund's mother told me Edmund has had to leave town! That he has been questioned by the Council on Public Safety and was afraid he might be arrested, and so he is trying to get to New York where he will be out of harm's way. And 'tis all your fault! Tell me the truth: You went to Mr. Kirby and told him Edmund is a spy, didn't you?"

It took Phoebe a moment to find her voice. "I told him I thought Edmund might be a spy. That some of his behavior had seemed suspicious to me. And—and—" Should she mention Nicholas's information? There was no point in keeping it secret now. "And Nicholas told me when he was here last that he had suspected Edmund all along. That he was here last summer trying to locate a spying ring in the city, and he knew Edmund had been part of it. So what I said to Mr. Kirby was right, after all."

Alice's mouth fell open at this statement, but Sarah scarcely seemed to hear it. "Phoebe, of all the mischief you have created in your life, this is the worst yet! How can I get it into your head that you have no business getting involved with all this political nonsense? All that is for men to worry about, not young girls without the sense God gave a fly! Here your sister might have had a brilliant future as a lawyer's wife, a *gentleman's* wife, and you've completely ruined it for her!

You've ruined Edmund's future in this town by spreading stories about him. He might have been arrested, and it would be all your fault! Now we can only hope he makes it safely to New York, traveling as he is between two armies. Either way, Alice might never be able to see him again."

Phoebe knew no loyalty to any political cause could console her mother for the loss of Alice's bright future. She was sorry for Alice, sorry for her mother, and even sorry for Edmund, but she could not repent her actions. She glanced back and forth from her mother to her sister. "What about George?" she managed. "He is with Washington you know, and Edmund's actions could have put him in danger. That battle at Trenton—Nicholas told me the Hessians were warned, and Edmund might have been the one to do it. What if George had been killed because the rebels walked into a trap?"

The image gave her mother a moment's pause, but she dismissed the possibility with a shake of her head. "Oh, Phoebe, don't be so dramatic. George is in danger because he insisted on joining the army instead of staying at home and helping his father the way he should have, but nothing Edmund did could have made it worse. If Edmund was a real threat to anyone, the men of the town would have discovered it without any help from you. Do you really think they need your help to run this war? Of course not! To tell the truth, it would have been a relief to me if this war had ended last month and your brother could have come home where he belongs. Now it will just drag on and on."

Seeing that her best argument had failed, Phoebe said nothing. Alice dropped down on the edge of the bed and wiped her tears with her handkerchief. Sarah gave Alice a compassionate and Phoebe a stern one.

"I think you owe your sister an apology. Not that anything can undo the mischief you have caused this time."

"I'm sorry, Alice," Phoebe began in a humble tone, and then she stopped. *What am I apologizing for? Did I really do wrong to report Edmund?* She tried to qualify her words. "I'm sorry you are so unhappy. I didn't mean to hurt Edmund. But I didn't want Edmund to put George and Nicholas in danger, or the other men in the army."

Alice blew her nose and pushed her hair back out of her face. "I hope this is a lesson to you, Phoebe. I hope you've learned how damaging your interference can be."

Phoebe escaped to the hall and her candlesticks, shamed and humbled. Sally glanced up from her sampler with one frightened, sympathetic look. Phoebe picked up her polishing cloth and began to scrub blindly, biting her lower lip. *I didn't mean to hurt anyone, Lord, truly I didn't. But I have to say, if I were in the same situation again, I would act the same way. If I was wrong, please show me—but I don't believe I was.*

She tried to keep out of the way for the rest of the day, hoping her mother's anger would expire before she could provoke her again. But when suppertime came the air in the kitchen was frigid. Sarah ignored Phoebe completely, and only spoke to her other children in a tense tone which escaped no one. Alice ate silently, her soulful blue eyes full of sorrow. Sally spilled the salt on the boardcloth and earned a sharp rebuke from her mother.

"What are you angry about, Mother?" Kit asked in an innocent voice, glancing around at his brothers and sisters.

Sarah was busy brushing the salt off the table. "Never mind. I can't discuss it. I don't know how I came to deserve such difficult children."

Phoebe winced at the implication of her mother's words. She glanced up and met her father's gaze from his seat at the head of the table. He gave her one sympathetic smile. Did he know the source of her mother's anger? Was it possible he didn't blame her the way her mother and sister did? Her spirits lifted a little.

After the supper dishes had been cleared and washed and put away, the rest of the family repaired to the parlor to sew and work and read, but Phoebe lingered in the kitchen with her knitting. She had already knitted a wool scarf for George and hoped Nicholas would be able to deliver it the next time he showed up at their door—if he ever came again. Now she was making a similar scarf for Nicholas, hoping it would be a suitable gift. She had not yet gotten up the courage to tell her mother the scarf was destined for Nicholas, knowing full well what her mother's reaction would be. She had nothing against Nicholas, but felt that Phoebe's attraction to him was both hopeless and unwise, and was keeping her from fully appreciating her luck with Miles Quincy. After all, a bird in the hand was worth two in the bush, or so her mother believed. So Phoebe had dual motives for keeping out of the way tonight.

She bent closer to the light from the single candle on the table, counted stitches and wondered what Nicholas would say when she presented the scarf to him. She would try to be as offhand as possible and had been planning her words for several days now. "You're like a brother to me, Nicholas, and I wanted to make a scarf for you as well." Would he believe her? She wasn't sure.

She looked up when the door opened and her father entered.

"You're all alone in here," he remarked with a quiet smile. "Why don't you join us in the parlor?"

Phoebe sighed and shook her head. "I think Mother might be happier if I stay out of sight."

Her father approached the table and sat on the bench across from her. "She told me why she is angry with you."

Phoebe looked up. "She did? She told you about Edmund?"

He sighed. "Aye. She is so disappointed for Alice's sake. It would have been a splendid match for Alice."

Phoebe watched her father's face in the flickering candlelight. "I understand why she and Alice are disappointed. But Papa, can you really believe I did wrong? Don't you understand that I couldn't let Edmund continue to spy against the rebel army? He was coming into our house, taking letters he believed had military information in them. All this while George is fighting for independence! How could I say nothing and let him continue?"

Her father was silent a moment, and Phoebe began to fear that he blamed her as well. Finally he spoke. "You are so different from your mother and Alice both, Phoebe. You have convictions that are bigger than your own family and your own circumstances. You have imagination; you are able to see the larger picture. Sometimes the price you have to pay is the anger of people who can't understand why you are taking the stand you are. People like your mother. I want you to obey your mother, of course, but you have to follow your conscience first."

Phoebe felt a flood of relief that at least one person in the family understood and sympathized. "Thank you, Papa." She groped for the words to express her heart. "I wish you could explain all this to Mother.

I wish you could explain why I acted the way I did. I hate having her so angry at me."

"She wouldn't understand." A brief silence fell between them, and he smiled at her again. "Be strong, Phoebe. You will be a better woman all your life for this experience."

಄ ಌ

After Edmund's escape, Phoebe wondered if she was likely to see Miles Quincy again. If Miles was only courting her because of Edmund's encouragement, he might lose interest when Edmund was no longer on hand to hearten him, since Phoebe believed she herself had given him as little encouragement as she could without being discourteous. Besides, she had no idea if Miles was aware of the role she had played in Edmund's problems. If he knew about that, he was very unlikely to ever call on her again.

Her hopes were dashed in the middle of January when he appeared at the door on a Sunday afternoon. Her mother called her down from her bedroom and left the two of them alone in the parlor with a pleased smile. Phoebe pasted a smile on her own face and determined to hide her dismay. She was used to him now and always planned a few topics of conversation in order to survive the hour without too much agony, but it was always work, never pleasure. Surely a courtship—even a very proper one—should be more enjoyable than this.

He seemed in comparatively high spirits and when he took her hand he actually kissed it. He had never done that before and she was not especially pleased, but she managed a smile as she withdrew her hand quickly. She led him to the settee.

"Tell me all your news. How is your mother? Is she in good health?"

That question usually provided about ten minutes of conversation, for Miles would tell her about his mother's health in detail and she simply had to nod and ask questions at appropriate points.

"My mother is doing well," he said, somewhat to her surprise. "This cold weather does not agree with her, of course, and she always ails a bit during the winter. But she is better this winter than in many years past. Last winter she had pneumonia. I believe I told you about her

126

pneumonia. She was in bed all winter with it, and we really feared for her life."

"Aye, I remember you mentioning that."

"She had a servant to care for her, but she didn't like the servant and wanted me to be with her all the time. I tried, you understand, but it was hard for me to care for my mother through that and also attend to my studies. I very much feared she would get the pneumonia again this year, with all the cold weather we've been having. But her health is really remarkably good this year. She is able to get out of bed and supervise the servants, which is a great help to me, you understand."

"Aye," Phoebe said. "I'm sure it is a great blessing that her health is so good."

He cleared his throat and wet his lips several times, and Phoebe began to wonder why he seemed so nervous and flustered. "I mentioned to my mother that I was coming to visit you, and she has a great desire to meet you."

"Oh!" Phoebe was momentarily speechless, taken aback. "That's very kind of her."

"I've told her a great deal about you, you understand. I've told her what a sweet, good-natured, pleasant, pretty young lady you are—" he almost stuttered on the last words, "and she said, 'Miles, I would certainly like to meet that young lady.'"

Startled, Phoebe felt her cheeks grow hot. She hoped, she prayed this conversation was not moving the way she suspected.

"It is very kind of you to say so," she managed.

It was a moment before Miles could bring himself to speak again. "I wanted to tell you that the date for my ordination has been set. It will be during the first week in March. After that I will be given a church. It will only be a small church at first, you understand."

Phoebe nodded with more enthusiasm than she felt, relieved that the subject had moved away from her personal charms. "That is very good news."

"Aye, and that is—and that is why I wanted to talk with you today." He took a deep breath; Phoebe felt her heart almost stop. "Now that I will have my own church, I will be in a proper position to marry. I think it is important for a minister to have a wife, to help him in his duties..." His voice trailed off as he glanced at Phoebe. She had no idea how she looked, but her face felt frozen. "And I would be very honored, Mistress Phoebe, if you would be my partner in my life's calling."

For a long moment Phoebe felt as if the air had been sucked out of her lungs. She simply sat and stared first at Miles, and then at the floor, and speech was impossible. She knew she must give some sort of an answer, and yet she was so completely unprepared.

"I am so very, very honored," she began, her heart pounding in her chest. "I truly didn't expect—" She glanced up at his anxious face and lowered her gaze again. Only one answer was possible, and she needed to give it, as simply as possible. "I am very, very honored that you would choose me, and I know you have a fine life to offer any girl. But it is impossible for me to accept right now."

The crackling logs in the fireplace echoed in the silence.

"Perhaps I have been precipitate." She could hear the trembling in his voice, and she felt very sorry for him. "I don't mean to rush you. Perhaps you need some more time to consider?"

Phoebe opened her mouth to agree. But that would be the easy way out. It would be cruel to give him false hope.

"I'm sorry," she managed miserably. "I never intended to give you false encouragement. I apologize if I did that without intending to. But Mr. Quincy, I really believe you should be courting some other girl."

&bo; &cs;

She escaped up to the bedroom after his departure and lay face down on her bed, hoping to cool her face in the quilt. The triumph of receiving an offer of marriage could not make up for the look of sadness and shock on his face as she said farewell. She knew now that her politeness, meant only as kindness, had given him false encouragement and ultimately compounded the pain of her refusal.

She lay on the bed for perhaps ten minutes, telling herself she had done the right thing, the only thing, that Miles Quincy would soon get over his disappointment and begin courting some other girl. She had given the only answer she could give. She couldn't have accepted him; she would have been miserable and would have disappointed him as well.

She heard her mother's voice at the door. "Phoebe? Are you in there?"

Her mother! Of course, she could never keep this from her mother. She sat up and scrubbed at her cheeks. "Come in."

Sarah entered the bedroom and studied Phoebe, a crease between her brows. "Did Mr. Quincy leave already? What happened, Phoebe?"

"He left." Phoebe studied the triangular pattern on the quilt.

"You didn't—you didn't—gracious, Phoebe, you didn't send him away, did you?"

"He asked me to marry him, and I told him I couldn't—I couldn't—" Phoebe couldn't continue.

"You foolish girl." Her mother's voice was less angry than she had expected, but rather sad and incredulous. She shook her head slowly in disbelief. "You foolish, foolish girl. The one decent suitor you have, and you throw him away, all because of some simple romantic notions. You'll never get another offer like this one. Never." Sarah turned and left the room, shutting the door behind her.

Phoebe lay down again on the quilt, torn between shame at her mother's words and relief that the lecture had been so brief. She thought of Nicholas then, his quick smile and his mischievous ways and his flashes of sympathetic understanding. All the longing she had struggled to contain for the last six months swept over her. If only Nicholas had been the one—but she was only a sister to Nicholas. He had said so on his last visit. *Maybe Mother is right. Maybe I've thrown away my only chance. But I couldn't marry Miles—even if I never get another offer. Even if Nicholas never wants me.*

ℬ Chapter Twelve ℭ

The winter seemed to drag on forever. It was cold outside, but Phoebe's discomfort from the bitter weather was intensified by the chill in the Fuller household. Alice attended to her duties in mournful quiet, and Sarah rarely spoke to Phoebe in a gentle tone. Phoebe wondered if she would ever be forgiven. She tried not to offend in smaller ways, to be more diligent than normal around the house, and especially to stay out of her mother's way. She spent most of her time with Sally and her brothers, helping with their lessons and chores. Whenever possible she escaped to visit Rhoda Kirby and her family, where she always found approval.

On one visit Mr. Kirby told his family the latest war news. The British and Hessians appeared content to remain east of the Delaware and no longer threatened Philadelphia, while the rebel army had moved into winter quarters north, in Morristown, New Jersey. Perhaps that was the reason she hadn't seen Nicholas in many weeks. She remembered him constantly and prayed for him every morning when she first opened her eyes. She prayed he was continuing to read his Bible and that he would spend time with other Christians in the army who could be an encouragement to him. In the evening she continued to knit on his scarf, and by the end of January it was finished. Sally told her it was very handsome and Phoebe privately agreed, all red, black, and white stripes. She wished she could give it to him, yet felt a bit nervous at the prospect.

Sometimes during the long, cold evenings, she sat up with a candle and her small collection of books, reading and rereading them. Her favorite was still *Pamela, or Virtue Rewarded,* and she read her favorite sections again although she had finished the entire volume during the summer. She would have felt foolish admitting that, as she read, she liked to picture herself and Nicholas as the characters in the book. The naughty, irrepressible Mr. B certainly reminded her of Nicholas in many ways. And virtuous Pamela was true to her principles and won her man in the end. She found comfort in the happy ending of the story, although she knew life did not always work out that way.

Toward the end of January she heard about him once through his sister. Lavinia wrote to thank Phoebe again for her role in the reconciliation and to tell her Nicholas had written to his family. Her father and Nicholas, Lavinia said, had not made any direct contact, but her father had heard of the meeting at Christmas and seemed relieved that Nicholas was alive and doing well. Lavinia, Charlotte, and their parents would be leaving for New York in February and would probably depart for England in early March when the worst of winter was past. Lavinia hoped Phoebe would write to her in England and keep them informed about Nicholas. Phoebe quickly wrote a reply and assured her friend that she would do her best.

By mid-February she had almost given up hope of seeing or hearing from him before the spring and sighed to think her lovely scarf would be wasted. But one unseasonably mild day she was scrubbing the kitchen floor when she heard a knock at the front door. She waited for Martha to answer it, but when the second knock sounded she rose and went to the door.

On the front step was Nicholas.

Her heart leaped at the sight of him, still so handsome, yet drooping and shivering from his long ride. She held the door wider for him. "Nicholas! Come in!"

He smiled as he stepped in the door and his glance swept over her. Phoebe realized with a sudden blush how she must look. She was wearing an old, stained petticoat, her hair had escaped in straggly tendrils from her cap, and she felt soiled and sweaty. She wiped her red, chapped hands on her petticoats. Why did she have to look so terrible when Nicholas showed up in town? Just like the day last July, at the State House!

"Let me call my mother," she told him, leading him into the parlor. "She's gathering in the wash, but she'll be here in a moment."

She called out the back door to her mother, then escaped up to her bedroom to change her petticoat, wash her face and comb her hair. When the mirror told her that her appearance was presentable, she returned to the parlor.

As Phoebe entered the room her gaze met Nicholas's and she thought she saw his eyes register a smile, either in approval or amusement at the change in her appearance. She was glad her mother was engrossed with a letter in her lap.

She chose a seat on the other side of him. "Did you bring my mother a letter?"

"Aye, a letter from your brother. I knew I was coming south and found a chance to ask him if he wanted to send word."

Phoebe sat next to her mother and glanced over her arm at the letter. "I know she's so happy to hear from George." And the letter would give Nicholas a warmer welcome than he might otherwise have found. "Is the army in Morristown now? You must have had a long ride."

"Aye, we're staying there for the winter. It took me longer to get here than it normally would have. I had to make a wide circle around the British army."

Phoebe gazed at him with compassion. "You must be so cold from your ride. Move closer to the stove and get warm."

He met her glance and smiled the smile she loved. "I'm plenty warm right now. It feels like heaven to be here."

Phoebe tried not to blush at his words. "I didn't think we would see you again until spring, until the army is on the move again."

He nodded. "Aye. I haven't needed to come to the city for a while, and I probably won't be here again soon. I'm only in town for this one night, and I have to start back again tomorrow."

Phoebe's heart fell at this information. But at least he was here for one evening. She wondered what business had brought him.

"Do you think your mother will let me stay the night here?"

"I'm sure she will." Phoebe looked to her mother for confirmation of the offer.

Sarah glanced up from her letter and nodded, but omitted a smile, and Phoebe suspected her mother felt less enthusiasm for the visit than she had in the fall. Perhaps she blamed Nicholas for Phoebe's refusal of Miles Quincy. Perhaps she believed Nicholas was sporting with her younger daughter, encouraging her infatuation. But really, it wasn't true. Ever since the one time he had kissed her last summer, he had never treated her as anything but a friend, by word or deed.

However her mother might feel about the visit, the rest of the family was excited by the news from George and pleased to have a guest for supper. When they gathered around the table Sarah permitted Phoebe to read the letter aloud to everyone. The two boys asked Nicholas many questions about life in the army, and the women shivered and pitied George as he told them about the wretched conditions under which the men were living.

"At least you aren't likely to fight any battles until the spring." Sarah refilled Nicholas's noggin with hot cider. "I hate to think of him cold and starving, but at least he won't be killed in battle."

"Thank goodness for the two battles we did win." Nicholas swallowed another gulp of the steamy fragrant brew. "Now if we can just get more supplies and ammunition by springtime, we'll be ready to take on the British again."

Phoebe nodded and leaned toward him, her eyes bright. "Mr. Kirby says that Congress is trying to buy supplies in Europe. That will make all the difference."

Nicholas grinned as he met her eyes. "I won't tell you what some of us in the army have to say about Congress, but I hope this time its actions are as good as its words."

"Enough melancholy talk about the war." Sarah rose from the table and began gathering up empty plates. "Come, Martha, don't dawdle. Let's get these dishes done and perhaps we'll have time for a little music. Alice, dear, we haven't heard you play the harpsichord in ever so long. I'm sure Nicholas would enjoy hearing you play."

"It would be delightful." Nicholas smiled at Alice, and Phoebe suppressed a tiny dart of jealousy. "I feel I'm truly back in civilization. First a delicious meal and now music." He threw an amused smile and a wink at Phoebe as he and Alice moved to the door.

"Phoebe, you help Martha with the dishes so Alice can play," Sarah ordered her daughter.

Phoebe swallowed hard but began to gather the dishes together as the rest of the family disappeared into the parlor. She filled the basin with hot water from the fire and washed faster than she ever had in her life as the tinkling sounds of the harpsichord drifted into the kitchen. Martha watched in amazement as she threw the dirty water out the back door and tossed her apron on the table.

In the parlor she found Nicholas standing by the harpsichord, watching Alice's graceful fingers on the keys. Phoebe hesitated until he glanced at her, smiled, and beckoned to her. Phoebe joined him, avoiding her mother's gaze.

"Perhaps your sister can play some of your Methodist hymns," he suggested to Phoebe at the next pause. "You sang a few to me that day last August—do you remember?"

Phoebe gave him a sideways glance and smiled archly. "Last August? I'm sure I cannot recall."

She would never forget anything about that day.

Alice immediately chose a hymn, while Sally, Kit and their mother joined the other two at the harpsichord.

"They are so different from the hymns I grew up with," Nicholas said. "They have such a modern, lively sound."

Phoebe grinned up at him. "Some of the tunes are tavern drinking songs. Maybe that's why they seem familiar to you."

Nicholas laughed. "What about that one you sang last August? I liked that one, but I don't remember how it goes."

"'Come ye that love the Lord,'" Phoebe suggested, and Alice began to play.

The hills of Zion yields a thousand sacred sweets
Before we reach the heavenly fields or walk the golden streets.
Then let our songs abound and every tear be dry,
We're marching through Emmanuel's ground to fairer worlds on
     high.

"I like that one," Nicholas said. "Sing it again, so I can learn it."

They all sang the song again, and the second time Phoebe quoted each line to him as it came up so he could sing along. She had never heard him sing before and was pleased with his rumbling baritone. Whenever he made a mistake she struggled to keep her composure, but finally at one particularly glaring error they both burst into laughter.

"Write the words down for me," he told Phoebe as the hymn ended, "that way I can carry them back to Morristown."

Phoebe rejoiced in seeing him so happy and content and comfortable with her family. It was almost like a little party, and she tried not to care that she had no private time alone with him. It was enough that Nicholas was here and she was able to stand beside him, singing with him and trying not to glow in the face of her mother's disapproval.

"I think it's time for everyone to go to bed," Sarah declared when the next song ended. "Come, Kit, Sally, we have a busy day tomorrow and it's past your bedtime." She threw Phoebe a pointed glance that indicated her adult daughters were included in the command.

Phoebe gave her mother a pleading glance in return. She was enjoying the evening with Nicholas so much, and the hour was not so late that they couldn't have sung a few more songs. But she didn't want to provoke her mother, especially in light of the tension that had existed between them in the last few weeks. She looked up at Nicholas with a last smile and turned toward the stairs, trailing Alice.

She expected him to follow them upstairs to the room he shared with Kit and Jonathan when he visited, but when she glanced over her shoulder she saw he had moved to the corner of the parlor where her father was sitting next to the Franklin stove. Her mother had disappeared into the kitchen. Phoebe saw Nicholas lean close to her father to speak to him, and though she couldn't hear the words, she saw her father nod and gesture to the seat next to him.

Well, that was odd. But how nice that Nicholas was making an effort to talk with her father. She would have loved to know what they were talking about, but probably wouldn't have a chance to ask him.

The next morning he breakfasted with the family and told them he needed to leave to return north. He met Phoebe's eyes across the table with a pointed look. She wasn't sure what he meant by it, but she was determined to find a moment alone with him, to give him his gift.

As soon as breakfast was over she whispered a few words to Sally, then ran upstairs to retrieve the two scarves from her chest. Nicholas would need to go to the barn for Syllabub, and so she decided her best chance of finding him alone was to meet him there. But to her surprise she found him waiting at the bottom of the stairs.

"I have something I want to give you before you leave," she told him, a little breathless.

He nodded as if pleased. "Can you come out to the barn with me for a minute?"

Phoebe fetched her cloak and followed him out the door, careful to avoid her mother in the kitchen. She clutched her gifts to her chest underneath her cloak. Outside the winter sun lit up the sky to an azure blue. The air was so mild, it was more like April than February.

"At least you have fair weather for your ride back to the army," she remarked as they stepped into the barn.

"Aye, the day was so fair yesterday, I thought spring was here to stay."

Phoebe shook her head. "I'm afraid we have more winter weather ahead of us."

"I fear you are right."

He closed the barn door and leaned against it, watching her expectantly, a half-smile on his face. Phoebe felt suddenly nervous and flustered.

"I made you a gift." She opened her cloak and held out the scarves, one in blue and yellow wool, the other in red and black. "This one is for George, and this is for you. I thought they might help keep you warm in this terrible cold."

"Why Phoebe, I'm honored. You made these?" He took the red and black scarf and unrolled it, then draped it around his neck. "The other men will be so envious, I'll need to make sure none of them steal it from me. And somehow I'll make sure this one gets to George."

Phoebe nodded, her face warm. She repeated the line she had been practicing for the last month. "I made one for George first, and I wanted to make one for you too, because you're like another brother to me."

She felt she had delivered her line with reasonable poise and started to breathe easier until she saw a look of surprise cross his face. Then he laughed. Phoebe felt her pink face turn red. Had she said the wrong thing? What was so funny? She bit her lip and turned away from him, but he was leaning against the barn door and she had nowhere to go.

"A brother?" He was still laughing. "Is that really the way you think of me, Phoebe?"

She found herself annoyed at his laughter and even more annoyed at herself. In spite of her efforts she had made a fool of herself anyway. Of course Nicholas knew she didn't think of him as a brother. He wasn't that blind.

"You were the one who said so," she returned, stepping away from him, but he reached out and caught her hand in his.

"I did? When did I say something like that?"

She remembered the words so clearly she was amazed he could have forgotten. "The last time you were here. You remember. You said you would defend my honor like a gallant brother if Miles ever forgets himself."

"Oh, that." The light dawned on his face, and he began to laugh again. "Now I remember. I was—I was actually remarking on something that Edmund Ingram had said to me once. One time when I met him and Miles and his friend Harry Hastings in a tavern." He seemed very amused by the whole situation, and Phoebe wondered why. For herself, she simply wanted to escape.

"I didn't know that." She spoke stiffly, trying to reclaim her dignity. She pulled her hand from his and stepped closer to the door, but Nicholas still wouldn't move from blocking it.

"So you think of me as another brother." He seemed determined to prolong the conversation as much as she longed to escape it. "Is that the way you thought of me last August? Or do you kiss all your brothers that way?"

She blushed more deeply at the memory of that day in the woods, but frowned to cover her embarrassment. "Of course not. I was wrong to act that way. But you weren't exactly behaving like a brother, either."

"Nay, that I was not," he admitted cheerfully. "So perhaps you can tell me which you prefer? That day in the woods, or the behavior of a good brother?"

Phoebe tried to pull herself up straight with a look of dignity. "The good brother, of course."

He laughed as if he disbelieved her and her cheeks burned again. He would never have laughed at Alice that way. "So if I tried to kiss you again, you would slap my face and tell me you never want to see me again."

She watched him warily, in confusion. "You wouldn't do that."

"Are you sure? Why do you think I asked you to come out here with me?"

She stepped back with a look of indignation and he laughed again. He reached for her arm but she stepped away from him, out of his grasp.

"Of course, that first kiss was before the charming Mr. Quincy came along," he continued. "Maybe he's responsible for your change of heart."

"You know he isn't." Phoebe felt a pang of dismay as she recalled Miles Quincy's proposal. She couldn't joke about Miles, even with Nicholas. Nicholas leaned down and caught her change of expression.

"Have you two come to a—an understanding?"

"Nay—" Phoebe began. "Aye—we have. I told him he needs to be courting someone else, and now my mother is angry with me."

"I see." She stole a look up into his face and saw the laughter disappear as he nodded. "She wanted you to marry him."

"Aye, but I couldn't. He was a good person, kind and decent and— but I didn't love him. I wouldn't have been happy. I tried, to make my mother happy, but I knew I wouldn't have been happy."

"You did the right thing."

"I know I did. But he was sad, and I feel bad about that."

Nicholas smiled again, but this time it was a tender, understanding smile. "You are soft-hearted, Phoebe, and I'm sure you would never deliberately hurt anyone. But Miles will get over it and be happy with someone else."

"I know."

"And you," he added in a softer tone, "you'll be happy with someone else too."

She looked up, met his gaze, and lowered her own. She felt her face grow warm.

"I won't be so vain as to think I made any part of your decision, but I don't want you to be mistaken about my feelings, Phoebe. I don't believe you are, but perhaps I should tell you myself."

She looked up into his face, hardly able to breath. He met her eyes, ducked his head, and seemed to be groping for words. "You have become very important to me, even though I have little to offer now and am not sure when, if ever, I could marry you. I may be killed tomorrow, or next month, or I may be wounded and lose a leg or an arm. It is impossible to know. I expect my father will disinherit me, and although I have a legacy from my grandfather, I may not be rich again for many years. But I do love you, Phoebe, and if that means anything to you, I hope you will be willing to wait for me."

It was unlikely that Phoebe, who was never the epitome of dignity or self-control in her best moments, should display either trait on such an occasion. She was never sure if he had pulled her close or she had fallen into his arms, but in an instant she was clasped in his embrace, as he followed up the first kiss from the night in the woods with a second, more solemn and tender and full of promise than any before it.

"I should tell you," he whispered against her hair, as they both paused to catch their breath, "since I'll never be able to carry you off by force, I decided I should talk to your father. We had a very pleasant conversation last night and he gave me his full blessing."

So that was the reason for him lingering behind the night before. Phoebe laughed then, the laughter bubbling up from a heart full of bliss and gratitude. "Why, Mr. B!" she exclaimed, "I never thought to hear such words come from your mouth! Are you actually going to turn into a respectable husband after all?"

Nicholas grinned at her, his eyes sparkling and crinkling at the corners in the way she loved. "My sweet, lovely Pamela." He leaned close to kiss her once again. "Perhaps there are times when virtue is rewarded after all."

31173584R00092

Made in the USA
Middletown, DE
23 April 2016